BACOPA
Literary Review 2022

Writers Alliance of Gainesville

ISBN: 13: 9798360641810

Printed in the United States of America

The views expressed in this collection—whether fiction, nonfiction, poetry, or prose poetry—are solely those of the authors and not necessarily shared by Writers Alliance of Gainesville or its members.

Cover Art: "Eye Sea" by Judi Cain. Standard, iridescent, and metallic acrylics on canvas. https://www.judicain.com

From the Editor

"Now and then, something holy allows a fresh budding."
—Sylvia Anne Telfer, "Listen to Gala's Mutterings"

Welcome to *Bacopa Literary Review* 2022. Our review is always published in autumn, and as I read and re-read each piece in the process of assembling the journal, I've come to feel that the fall is indeed a fitting time of year to send our little ship of words out into the world. We are proud to offer once again a kaleidoscope of authors in terms of age, range of experience (both overall life experience and as writers), ethnicity, country of origin, and place of residence. Our 2022 crew of contributors is truly international, including folks who hail from or reside in Africa, East and South Asia, Latin America, North America, and Europe.

Here in North Central Florida, in the middle-sized university city and its surrounding environs of woods, spring-fed rivers, and gently rolling hills which our editors and the members of our organization, the Writers Alliance of Gainesville, call home, fall is often an odd, overlapping time of year. The seemingly-endless Florida summer is grafted onto our brief but sometimes surprisingly sharp winter by an even briefer season that all too often feels like it lasts only one month—either October or November—rather than three. Our bustling college burg is set in a region where the true subtropics of the peninsula begin to shift towards the more temperate zones to the north. Yankee and Midwestern friends are shocked when I tell them that we usually get at least a few hard freezes here in the winter. "And you're in *Florida*!" they muse.

The many clashing realities of Florida—from its brutal history of colonization and slavery, to its picture-postcard presentation as the ultimate vacation playground for the striving working class and the idle rich alike, from its glimmering jewel-blue springs to its sweltering vast, swampy prairies—are simply another expression of the complexities and contradictions any old place in the world carries with it. At least, that is, in the minds of the humans who inhabit and help shape it for each other, or pass through it, carrying away with them images and impressions molded by their own individual histories.

Reading through the selections that have come together to make up this year's edition of our journal, I find myself fascinated by the way that all artists, but writers perhaps most of all, take up and add to the crazy-quilt that is our experience of this world. In some ways writing is our most direct way of communicating not only clear, specific thoughts—allegedly direct communications from the rational foreground of one individual mind to another—but also feelings, images, and impressions, the murkier, less-direct, more pliable elements of examined existence.

Autumn is a time of reflection—the hazy, heavy gold light of summer turns almost imperceptibly to the silver coin of winter, prompting glances cast backward across the maze of days that made the months leading up to it. These pages offer backward glances aplenty, from the elegy-as-social-commentary of Shauna Osborn's Formal Poetry prize-winning poem "Amelia's Freckle Cream," to the laugh-along kitchen table confessional of Victoria Lynn Smith's Honorable Mention Humor essay "Show and Tell to Remember."

Autumn is also a time of melancholy. As Halloween, All Hallows, Samhain, the Day of the Dead, and other autumnal traditions remind us, fall is a kind of premature funeral for the year, foretelling its death in the depths of winter. This sense of what we lose each fall is beautifully expressed in Jennifer Overturf's haiku triad, "Growing Season." As some of our award winners and other contributors clearly show through their work, pain, darkness, and struggle are still on many people's minds, despite the notion that the worst of the COVID-19 pandemic is now behind us. The heartbreak of the Russian invasion and war in Ukraine is relayed with painful immediacy and urgency in Taras Bereza's "There's No Way Back Home to Mariupol." The ongoing legacy of family trauma amid poverty and struggle weighs heavy in Murzban F. Shroff's Fiction Award winning story, "An Act of Kindness." But fall weather and the invitation it extends to lure us out of doors can also be a gentle, even joyful sort of forecast, a harbinger of death in some sense, yes, but as resonant, as telling and as graceful as the metaphor employed in Julie McNeely-Kirwan's "The Nighttime Car."

Autumn can be a time of playfulness and trying new things too, from Halloween costumes to the new cool-weather clothes that, yes, even here in North Florida, we must sometimes wear. This year, we've broadened the scope of the journal by expanding our usual Poetry category, dividing it into Free Verse and Formal Poetry and adding the new category of Visual Poetry. Our choice to include this hybrid genre reflects the vision of our new Poetry Editors Reinfred Addo and Oliver Keyhani, while also honoring the genre-blending, experimental legacy of longtime Editor in Chief and outgoing Associate Editor Mary Bast and former editor-of-many-hats Kaye Linden. This expansion of both the girth and variety of contents in *Bacopa* coincides with and echoes the broader feeling of expansiveness in our world today as we continue to emerge from over two years of dealing with COVID. The sense of simmering excitement, of burning hope for renewal, that many are feeling these days, even as the nights grow longer and the air cools, is exemplified in the flip side of many of our cultures' autumnal traditions. As we prepare for one year to pass, we anticipate the sun-warmed coming of the next growing season, burning Samhain bonfires and lighting the myriad glimmering lamps of Diwali.

The intense mix of mourning and anticipation of change is reflected in some of the responses to our poetry editors' call for works addressing the impact of the pandemic and other health issues in communities of color. It shows up in a muted shade in Free Verse Honorable Mention winner Sunyoung Kay's haunting "In the Name of the Name." A louder version of this same mix is distilled like the very fire that invades the narrator's bones in Neethu Krishnan's searing Creative Nonfiction prizewinner, "Girl Sunsplit." Even as she lies bedridden by a debilitating illness that paralyzes her with pain in the Indian summer heat, Krishnan flashes back to an image of herself in earlier days, striding evanescent with joy in a sequined skirt: *I'm invincible, ethereal; chipping the gilded sun to confetti, a million iridescent coins spring forth from me.* Dear reader, may you carry that spirit of shining joy with you through all the pages that follow, and into the year to come.

—J.N. Fishhawk

J.N. Fishhawk	Editor in Chief
Mary Bast	Associate Editor
Tessa Walters	Managing Editor
Alec Kissoondyal	Fiction Editor
Stephanie Seguin	Creative Nonfiction Editor
Stephanie Seguin	Humor Editor
Oliver Keyhani	Poetry Co-Editor
Reinfred Dziedzorm Addo	Poetry Co-Editor

Bacopa Literary Review 2022 Prizes

FICTION
Award
An Act of Kindness / page 65 / Murzban F. Shroff
Honorable Mention
Benny & Bjorn / page 27 / Lilia Snowfield Anderson

CREATIVE NONFICTION
Award
Girl Sunsplit / page 50 / Neethu Krishnan
Honorable Mention
Waiting / page 85 / Miki Lentin

HUMOR
Award
How Busy I Was / page 149 / Marjorie Drake
Honorable Mention
Show and Tell to Remember / page 21 / Victoria Lynn Smith

FREE VERSE POETRY
Award
Listen to Gala's Mutterings / page 70 / Sylvia Anne Telfer
Honorable Mention
In the Name of the Name / page 136 / Sunyoung Kay

FORMAL POETRY
Award
Amelia's Freckle Cream / page 13 / Shauna Osborn
Honorable Mention
All Love Poems Are Horror Poems / page 69 / R. Thursday

VISUAL POETRY
Award
A Change in Mood II / page 7 / Karla Van Vliet
Honorable Mention
NEWS / page 33 / J. Nishida

Contents

FICTION

CREATIVE NONFICTION

HUMOR

FREE VERSE POETRY

FORMAL POETRY

VISUAL POETRY

The Taste of Hundred-Leaved Grass

Marisca Pichette

To understand me, you must first understand my land.

In my house I hear coyote songs, sharp howls crumbling into a diminuendo of barks and yips. The first howl is to find. Where is the family? Where are the children? Come here, come let me show you what I have found. Let me share.

The second howl is the answer. Here we are, here I am. Call me again, and I will come.

Bark, yip, hello. Coyote summons coyote and they converge in sound.

When the song begins I sneak out into the darkness to better hear their concert, reintroductions across relations. Hello, brother. Hello, sister. Grandmother, cousin, child. We sing together to join together, to hunt together, to feast together.

The concert rises then falls, comes to an echoing close that I can still make out, if I am quiet. I must be careful when I open and close the door. Too loud, and the music stops. I stand on the porch wrapped in my breath and listen until it is silent. If they are close I feel like I am part of the song, another detail in the orchestra of night. A flashlight's determined beam might catch their eyes, watching me watch them.

When I was very young the coyotes came down right next to my house. Pre-dawn light caught their grey bodies rolling in and out of the woods, wild waves borne on a current only they knew. Their silence was more unnerving than their song.

One paused and looked up at the house, at the window, at me. Eyes I couldn't make out, an expression my upbringing failed to equip me with the tools to comprehend. The coyote turned away from me and followed the eddies of its pack, and the sun rose.

A coyote is fierce and afraid. Say a word and it flees, seeking refuge in the woods that protect it with the colors of its fur. When I hear them, I cannot see them. When I see them, we are both silent as the grass.

Over the years I've amassed a handful of coyote pictures. Using the digital Canon my parents got for me one Christmas I zoomed in, tracking their movements those few times they chose to emerge, skirting the field at daybreak and day's end. They are the color of dead and dying leaves: grey, brown, gold, russet, beige. Even in the tall grass they seek to blend in, moving with a liquidity I could never match. A coyote in silence is an opportunity, cautious and ephemeral.

Despite the filtered, fortunate photos on Instagram, I am no expert on wildlife. Lynx, coyotes, turkeys, deer, foxes—all the subjects of my awed observation. My knowledge of their private lives reaches only to the edge of the woods. Their thoughts are not available to me. I watch them as I watch the stars—at a distance I can little comprehend, and know I'll never narrow.

I have sat by my house for two decades, observing and recording, ogling and listening, smelling and exhaling. A question sliding through my mind finds no true purchase, is answered in its basest form by Audubon's book on New England wildlife.

To understand, approach my words like the coyote's song.

Knowing nothing, forgetting to ask.

***

My land is not my land.

One acre holds the home of my childhood, owned and maintained by my parents. The miles around, the wild trees, are owned by my neighbor. She never cared that my constant exploration took me through and through her woods, ignoring the Private Property notices as I followed my self-appointed path. Woods that fell to her care from her parents, woods she was content to ignore.

On the hill: the orchard.

There are two orchards, both owned by the Clarks. The first is a peninsula, surrounded on three sides by the woods. This is the elder orchard, ancient apple trees twisted with age and wisdom. Here I once found a skeleton. Raccoon? Opossum? I don't know. I wrapped the skull in my scarf and brought it home.

The second orchard buzzes year-round. Apples, plums, peaches, cherries, blueberries, pumpkins, pears. This is my destination.

I have a canvas satchel that I am filling. The sides are stained with ink— walnut brown, purple. In it I put my journal, a wrapped pouch of hermit cookies, a water bottle, a cylinder. Also within: dried yarrow in a small wood box tied with leather. Sheep's wool. A bottle of ink. Its top is an eyedropper.

Outside it is spring. Fifty degrees, sunny and full of the smell of thawing. I pull black boots onto my feet and wear a sweatshirt. My hair finds its way into a bun as I am not committed to trying anything harder.

When I go to the orchard I carry as little as possible. It's a hike through the woods, up the rutted dirt path carved out by tractors and pickup trucks pulling carts of apples, peaches, pears. In the summer I walk a cloud of dust.

The hill has a name: Turtle. I don't know where this name came from, but from Turtle Hill I can see Wekwamps, which the colonists call Sugarloaf. This is because its blunted head looks like a loaf of sugar that has been worn down from a cone. I used to teach with loaves like that, back in my museum educator days. I used to hold them in my hands and tell the story of Wequamps and the Pocumtuck who named him. Stories, one half-hour at a time, one school group at a time.

I wonder how many students remembered my words after they left the smoke-scented museum, a monument to centuries of mistakes. Did they see how memory stretched into the present, bodies crossing lands named and renamed again? Or did they only recall the funny clothes, the unfamiliar smells?

I imagine the Pocumtuck named my hill, too. Turtle.

The Pocumtuck, whose memories recorded Lake Hitchcock, and the forming of our world. Memories I learned from living descendants, passed on as best I could. The people of Turtle Island. The world on the turtle's back.

I am walking today to reach that island, access that memory.

My first hurdle is the brook, a little sliver of water that pools at the side of my house, dug deeper and dammed by my father when I was younger. He created that depth so my sister and I could dip our toes in the cold water in summer. Seasons since and silt has washed down to reclaim that pool. I hop over the trickle and begin to climb.

Not far into the woods I come to the rusted trailer. Two wheels on a triangular frame that I can see from my house. This landmark has stuck in my mental map because it doesn't belong, has never belonged. And because it doesn't belong so much, it has always belonged. It is there to be the thing that doesn't fit, the reminder of how this landscape has been altered, tinkered with, held.

I walk around steel bones and continue up. My path is on the edge of the forest. Where I walk the trees are still young, no wider around than my hips. They have been planted and grown in the decades since this was farmland. Pausing to look back at my house through the trees, I see the footprint of my home from an elevated point. Where my house is there used to be a stage-coach inn. Years of my father's metal detecting in the yard yielded five-gallon buckets full horseshoes.

The grass hides the memories beneath.

Leaves crunch under my feet as I climb higher, my satchel bouncing against my thighs. On my right the earth climbs higher, heading into the deeper woods that lead to Shelburne and the power lines. On my left the hill flattens into a field, the rubble of a stone wall separating me from the grass.

I walk in this liminal zone, sometimes finding level ground, othertimes climbing further. My sights are set ahead. Through the trees I can see the place where the forest ends and Turtle Hill begins.

I step out into the sun. Apple trees greet me, white blossoms scattered through the green of their leaves. I walk between the first trees until my boots find the dirt road. Tire tracks from the trucks that tend these trees break me from my transcendental plane, remind me that no part of the wilderness I explore is wild. Has it ever been?

I follow the road in a gradual incline until it splits. On my right the hill that holds the forest continues to rise east, inclining around a lesser-used path. Through the mousehole-like opening I can glimpse the old orchard, its grandmother trees that still bear apples every year. In a different mood I might walk that direction, but today I am following a line, and I turn away. I climb Turtle Hill.

Humidity breaks and reforms around me. The road is cold with spring mud, my feet slipping as they search for purchase. I am not graceful when I climb. I stumble, my satchel flails, and I know I will be sore tomorrow from this simple exertion. Every time I make this pilgrimage I tell myself I will do it more often. Every time, I forget the moment I depart how to keep that promise to myself.

Slowly I advance, my boots spattered with mud, my socks damp. Sweat holds my shirt to my ribs, my leggings to the backs of my knees. I swat early mosquitos away as the white dots of apple blossoms change to the soft pink of plum and peach. Their fragrance is something I feel in my memory but cannot ever recall fully, like the first tentative touch of sun after winter.

Panting, I know my journey is almost done. I almost jog the last dozen feet to where the incline levels into a domed slope. I leave the muddy road for the wet grass, stringy and tufted around each tree, solemn attendants to sprawling mothers of many. I pick an aisle; something tells me this is the same aisle I pick every time, the one before me that seems to lead to the edge of the world.

On either side, pink and green and dew. Ahead—the curving of grass, the distance of the forest continuing after this hill is complete. I know that if I kept walking I would eventually reach the Deerfield River. Every time I come I think that one day I will go all the way.

Between these trees I lower myself, let my leggings become wet through with dew and the memory of frost. I swing my satchel around onto my lap and open it. I take out each item. My water bottle. I take a long gulp, realizing how thirsty the trip has made me. The hermit cookies, wrapped in a cotton napkin. I untie the bundle and eat one, looking around as I chew. This is when I imagine I am somewhen else, somewhen long ago. Another gulp of water to wash the crumbs down.

I remove the ink, the cylinder, my journal. My journal is red leather, unlined. Drops of ink stain the cover along with the raised scars of melted and hardened wax. When I open it the binding utters a faint creak that holds me where I want to be, where I imagine being.

Pulling the lid from the cylinder, my quill pen slides with a hiss into my hand. It is red like wine. When I open my ink I am careful to set it on a flat section of the ground, nestled in between tufts of half-dead, half-revived grass. Liquid shadows reflect the sky.

I open to blank pages. I have no plan of what to write. A story? A letter? A memory? Or do I write about this trip, about leaving and arriving, sitting in shade that is just a little too cold in early spring? I dip my pen and begin with no conception of how I'll end.

Each page must dry fully before I continue. I sit, wait, breathe the season. Somewhere, something is buzzing. I listen and try not to think about how wet my butt is. The page dries, and I turn it.

After a while I finish whatever Turtle Hill told me to write. The last page stops reflecting the light and I close my journal, return it to my satchel. Back in goes the ink, the cylinder that holds my quill. I have one more hermit cookie and one more gulp of water. These, too, go back. I hold the box of yarrow in my hands. I have no bug bites, no scrapes yet. I place the box back into the bag next to the wool.

With my satchel filled and buttoned I stand, shaking the cold from my legs. I walk back along the path I chose but do not descend, yet. Instead I come around in front of the trees and look down.

The orchard is spread out below us, the peaches and I. White-blossomed apple trees in row upon curving row. Pines across the road, casting shadows. Four ancient willows bowed over a green pond.

From Turtle Hill I listen to cars drive past, to the distant hum of the highway. I look out and see Wekwamps, his head and broken neck connecting to the slope of his shoulders, rolling along the horizon to his flat tail. I imagine Lake Hitchcock between us, glacial waters dammed by Wekwamps' lodge. I wonder about the lake's first name, inherited and erased and alive in the bloodlines that connect to that past.

When I have finished with looking I turn away from the valley and begin my descent. I walk into and out of my imagined past, a history I've pieced together from my childhood and the stories that passed through me.

The song of Turtle Hill echoes behind me, but I don't hear the lyrics.

***

The contents of my satchel empty onto the counter. I put everything away, returning hermit cookies to their Tupperware; journal, ink, and quill to their desk. Timeless things have anachronistic places, accessed and abandoned in waves. Before I leave my satchel I reach inside, remove the box of yarrow.

I untie the leather strap. Grey-green leaves, shriveled, smelling faintly of summer, faintly of dust. I break off a piece and dab it between my teeth. When I chew, my saliva reawakens the life within and the leaf unfurls.

One mosquito bite, warm and yellow on my hand. I pull the yarrow from my teeth and grind it into the welt.

The itching will stop soon.

A Change in Mood II
Karla Van Vliet

Transition
Angeline Schellenberg

After the painting "Transition" by Angela Lillico

Lampshade evening.

A heron lifts
from the far bank,

its crowbar lit red
by diminishing sun.

In my phone a million
thistles blur

without a butterfly.

We love to say
the lake is glass—

we need a mirror
we can enter.

The Gelid Teals of Thunder
David M. Alper

marsh and sinew in the evening

when the thunder spills over the city

or lightning fires round some country way

or bends light, or the storm works out

the hard nonsense of waiting

for love to touch their cheek

or pass over the train tunnel

into the future's cracked seam.

We walk out on the spring streets

and sway,

muscling our moccasins

though the world is corduroyed

and we reach for the next step

in the way that we sometimes fall

to speak to each other.

Santorini Blue

Karin Hedetniemi

In one of the photos, you are reading a book on the terrace. I can't see the cover. You are smiling. There's nothing on the table — no cup of coffee, no glass of wine. It must be midday. It must be before the plunge pool. I have no recollection of this.

But that deep blue sky. It was the bluest blue, painted on church domes and doors. The deep twilight sky. The Aegean Sea cupping us in open palms.

***

Strange, I remember with such clarity an ordinary moment of bliss: sitting in our backyard on a frosty spring morning, steam rising from our coffee cups, the sky a soft blush. Listening to birdsong, welcoming the day, peacefully and unhurried.

I examine the next photo. The steps, oh there were steps! Donkeys carrying heavy packs as if nothing had changed in hundreds of years.

I forget what we brought inside our heavy suitcases — the last time we ever travelled with them. Embarrassed to have the porter carry our ridiculous bags down two hundred winding steps, then up again upon our leaving. He had hoisted both boulders on his shoulders, a weightlifting feat of strength, and we followed behind, ashamed. I forgot the shame of travelling with all our stuff.

Inside our rented cave home, I remember how coolness enveloped us. I study the photo. A vase on the wooden plank table. One unopened pink peony, paired with one softly fading pink rose, beginnings and endings. A bowl of fruit: two apples, one orange, one lemon.

Next, my first photographed impressions of the village from the perspective of our terrace. Bright pink bougainvillea blossoms spilling over whitewashed ledges. The odd home painted dusty rose, sandy yellow, but all other buildings brilliant white. The Greek flag flowing proudly in the marine breeze.

Daytime, I recall the narrow streets were wall-to-wall bodies. Bodies pressing into my back, their sweaty skin touching my sweaty skin. The urgent swell and push of the crowd needing to take it all in — just a few frenzied hours to enter and exit every shop, thread the village.

We would retreat down those two hundred steps. Hide from the hot sun and hot people.

this cave with smooth, curved walls
cool, serene, calm, quiet
a place without sound
warm honey wood, sunlight
on our wet swimsuits and towels, drying
on the terrace
the old church bell, silent and still

****

Late afternoon, with the cruise ship day-trippers gone, I could finally see the smooth cobblestones underneath my feet. Notice doorsteps adorned with potted hibiscus and olive trees. Little pots of succulents, herbs.

In this photo, there's a café with old wooden chairs on a decorative tile floor, windows embracing the sea. Then, a bakery. I forgot about those marvelous small bakeries with gorgeous pastries — golden threads of sugar piled high on warm baklava.

There's a bookstore with beautiful paperbacks about birds and the sea, sleeping in an old leather suitcase outside the door.

Now a gift shop with olive wood crucifixes and gilded religious icons. Decorative boxes, bowls, and figurines. Miniature carved donkeys carrying someone else's tiny heavy pack.

I forgot how the wind billowed my sundress and brushed my bare toes.

my toes peeking out of the plunge pool
your toes touching my toes
your favorite plaid shirt
the purity of my love
inside the blue sky
of our future

****

To fill in more memory gaps, I search back in my emails for dispatches sent home. I wrote that you spotted a peregrine falcon flying over the cliffs. You were excited. I don't remember the falcon. I don't remember this moment at all.

But just now, I remember faces and long shadows during the golden hour.

We were sitting on our little cliffside terrace, with hundreds of sunset gazers lining the embankment at the top, annoying me with their peering cameras. Voyeurs looking into our private patch of paradise.

During our previous ten days on Crete, I'd written pages of detailed journal notes, capturing every sensory experience of that place and time. But in Santorini, I'd jotted a solitary, cryptic line. *Plunge pool x 2. Souvenirs. Fireworks at 11 pm - woke us up.*

I don't remember the fireworks.

From Crete, I brought home so many souvenirs. An olive wood bowl. Painted ceramics. A necklace made of seed pods I bought from an old man with a long beard. He called them *God's tears*. You took a photo of us. I've looked at that photo so many times. Worn that necklace every summer since.

How is it, I didn't buy any souvenirs in Santorini. Maybe that was part of the forgetting. No touchstone to hold, trigger memories, inspire storytelling. Just these digital images, stored away for a decade, that now seem like someone else's life.

Memories, like digital photos, change slightly each time we access them.

Looking at these photos for the first time in ten years, it strikes me: this is the closest I'll ever come to reliving Santorini, exactly as it happened. At least, as it was photographed. Each time I revisit these photos, the pixels of my memories will change.

The rest of them are already gone.

What I remember more is the ordinary bliss of everyday life. That short time, we had together.

the dog's tail starting to wag
five minutes before
you pull into the driveway
pulling your blue plaid shirt
out of the laundry basket, still warm
as I fold it, warm against my chest
your toes touching my toes
sunlight
cloudless blue sky
expansively full
of things I've let go

***

Amelia's Freckle Cream

Shauna Osborn

The internet is always in need of a new meme
and vanity skips no one, not even Amelia Earhart–the famous female aviator,
whose body was identified near Howland Island by a pocketed vial of aged freckle cream

Someone fervently revered and known to have little squeam,
Amelia saw her own speckled skin as a constant humiliator,
and, well, the internet is always in need of a new meme.

Couldn't imagine that part being "the dream,"
particularly years after the pilot's prep to match a bird's soar,
for her body to only be marked hers by that trusty vial of freckle cream.

Humiliation being part of the downfall, an unending reminder of theme,
like that obligatory picture of Kate Winslet hogging the damned Titanic door.
Jesus, the internet needs a new meme.

We're all metal buckets, leaking, frayed somewhere along the seam,
watching footage of the uprising marches, hearing the voices of ignited loved ones roar,
"Will you be identified only by your favorite facial cream?!?"

Advertisers have won the war, full domination no longer a scheme.
Consumption required for decades by all technological/audio/screen manipulators.
The vast and commodified internet is always in need of a new meme,
full up with once darker bodies identified only with stylish vials of designer freckle fade cream.

Haiku for One Lone Soul

Paula M. Rodriguez

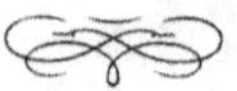

Inside this black hole,
no sound, no light, no beating–
only one lone Self.

Moon on the tarot–
a trail of bizarre choices
ends in a mirage.

Another red dawn
rising to the West of dust.
I'll write back to Earth.

A longshoreman sings
as the dying sounds of port life
caress the South wind.

A caesarean where God leaves the scalpel in my mother's belly

Sarpong Osei Asamoah

The rain is a miscarriage without the blood

My mother wanted a daughter
And instead God gave her rain in August.

Don't get me wrong,
Rain is beautiful even when it burns the eyes.

Perhaps my tears are the horns of dying animals.
Maybe the scalpel would mourn me if it wasn't bleeding too.

There is an etch in my roof the size of God's mouth—
My sister's blood leaks through it.

My mother's womb, a bell with no speaking voice.
She, bitten by the white page teeth of an anesthetic;

A chemical so silent the nurse held it like it was God.
The thumb of the syringe pressed against my mother's throat

Asking her to die long enough for my unborn sister to resurrect.
We all came into the world like this—on a sailing boat at a knife's edge.

My mother reads this little red email,
She, a red stone that has language.

If blood could speak, It would be the sign language of clot.
And everyday, somewhere near my blood, a red stone stops rolling.

Everyone Knows Where They're Going

Kateri Kosek

It may as well begin here, in a place without him: a small gallery back home in the Northeast, my face so close to his massive painting that the sharp lines blur. He is in Romania—always laughably far away—making more paintings.

I want so badly to see the one he made from the photo I liked (for me, I like to think)—the shining concrete floor of that factory on the outskirts of that Midwestern city, him snapping photos while I chatted up the old-timer who showed us around. (Lit up when I said Boston, New York, but knew better than to get lost in such places. Everyone in the city knows where they're going, he said.) Industrial fans whirred. Plastic dust stuck to the old machines like snow.

For two weeks we poked around warehouses, stood around in kitchens. I cooked him meals from the farmer's market. Roommates by chance, we stayed up late, sipped double IPAs in a town that drank Busch Light, as freight trains piled up along the Missouri.

At midnight he'd rise with a casual good night my dear, scrupulous about bedtime, and everything else.

I fall in love with the vacancies he paints—shuttered factories, the clean lines of machines I have no name for. I write about Nebraska, about silos and corn and the humming gears of that factory, and of course it is all about him.

Then, two days before he leaves, he begins to cry. We're sitting at the kitchen table. He says girlfriend with an air of apology. In the beleaguered tone of revealing something inevitable. She is leaving for some time, this partner of a decade, a long time in a faraway place, and he is scared.

I didn't know you had a girlfriend.

No one ever asked.

Usually it comes up.

She's flying in tomorrow to drive home with him, and this, the precious night she will rob us of, bothers me more than the fact of her existence.

Unburdened, he looks at me differently that night. We talk about provocative things while sitting on separate couches. He hugs me in passing, our last night alone, almost long enough for it to mean something.

When he drives to Omaha to get her, I steer my bike to the tracks, stare at the hypnotic crush of wheels.

He kisses me on the cheek and promises to visit and soon, from Beijing, sends anguished emails and grainy neon photos, and reading them, I breathe in China's lurid dust, wishing we were back in his rented car, hightailing it to Kansas City to race through art museums and watch the Royals play in 95-degree Midwestern heat, darting around between Lincoln, Omaha, cities whose names dripped with America, far from our lives.

He visits once. Theorizes at length on platonic relationships like it has nothing to do with us. He invites me to Boston and I dream of rolling in to South Station, of rushing through the strange city not knowing.

Instead, I invite myself to Utica in the coldest week of winter to catch one of his shows; wait five hours for him to arrive. I walk up Genessee Street as far as I can, cowboy boots slipping on snow-packed sidewalks. It grows dark, the establishments thin out and I loiter in a gas station to get warm, pull a peanut butter sandwich from my bag, and turn around.

Later that night in a bar filled with drunk college students he complains about the untrusting girlfriend in Spain, then back at the hotel, goes to sleep while I lie awake all night at the edge of his small bed he allows me to sleep in, Hotel Utica hung with chandeliers and reminiscent of glory, a time of white pillared lobbies when presidents motored along the Erie Canal to get here, and upstate New York mattered.

After that I stop trying. Probably I was one in a string of scrupulous, emotional affairs he, a hopeless romantic, courted across the globe. Only now can I appreciate it for what it was—a spell that could neither be broken nor maintained. A noble exercise in the power of the unsaid.

I've already seen this painting. He paints it again and again—the stilled machines, the tarnished light spilling through empty stairwells, these things that amount to nothing but take up whole walls, so gloriously obsolete.

Found, please bring along an I.D. to claim

John Agbaeze

In the morning, I'm perched on an old wooden chair, chewing on the

words of the radio announcer, and as usual, a hawk cak-cak-caks, as if

telling the fate of all the people who happen to fall, even here.

I could tell what a realist the hawk was, for in the fullness of time, nothing has

ever been salvaged that fell. The announcer knows, so the tone dangled

between shaky and outright loss. The morning chimes at half its pace,

collecting sighs, however little. On some timeshift, conviction is in the transition
of dawn to dusk, yet,

Genesis might stay longer should Moses have chosen for it. My eyes read its
stares and wished they knew the hawk's song.

Once I lost a sneeze, I looked to the sun to grab a sneeze, eyes wide open, but

twitched when I couldn't stretch a hand, trembling from its own inability to
reach for a leaf, to hold onto the comfort of the glorious amber circle.

I remember the dread of an accompanying loss, how I woke the night up,

grilling it with rhetoric and the specifics of being an unfortunate. My
language was extant, carrying an I.D. to

I.D., if fortune smiled on me, the relics of shadowy sighs. The announcer,

howling their voice to the sibilant loneliness of a hush, agrees. This one isn't
any more special than the others; unfortunates of a pus society, lost to the

craze of nonchalance. Everyone knows another loss is not a creation. It took only two months to sail past the slimness of a police stray bullet in the skull of

Kenneth. Loved ones say he was a dove. He would rather crawl onto his peace than snooze on a jolt.

We lost empathy in the corners of our streets. I pointed to a street and told a stranger how it, the street, built an enclave

and harbored the soul of their eggs. Territory that ripped the night with lights,

co-owned the fabrics woven into the strands of each structure.

Everyone knew where to find a balm for their rusty hopes and some creaks,

until the soul left the body, raped. The eggs sauntered onto their dead, carrying

their heads in pains. Their shells stand as a memorial where the old liberty bell

once stood and tolled, moribund and beauty-less. I find the thin line between living and existing and

the announcer's voice launches a series of fluid upthrust. I never hiccuped

under duress, but what's with this spasmodic inhalation brokered between a

closed glottis? I don't want to score yet another naught in my attempt to wake up.

Over the radio is something: *found, please bring along an I.D. to claim.* I wonder

if they sought after validation. Here, nothing falls, decays, and wears a new skin. They decay into loss. I've stayed lain,

dead and unwilling, just so I don't wake to the direness of day. I stopped expecting a breakthrough when bullets broke through flags and casually took fall.
Bloodied trails and shattered flesh. But if truly found, please, will me unto

salvation, unto the ascent of the hawk. If bringing along an I.D. to claim, let me

forget the smell of my bedsheet. I will guide the length of the year like the stretches of its sun in the day and the moon of its night.

I will say this is the day neither the sun nor the moon slipped through the horizon without a want. If found truly, the osiers blackmailing the day's claim

to wholeness, the excesses of an identity card to validate relief are only a few punched buttons.

Deliver up the lost, unscathed. Confidence, too, unlost.

Show and Tell to Remember

Victoria Lynn Smith

Inside my dress pocket, I had the best thing for show and tell. In 1964, I was new at Pleasant View Elementary, and having started in October instead of September, I was an outsider. My kindergarten classmates were going to be impressed. The popular girls would envy me and ask me to jump rope with them during recess. The cute boys would elbow each other and try to sit by me at snack time. My pretty teacher, with bouncing brown hair that flipped up in a long continuous curl around her neck, would look at me with approval.

"Vickie," the teacher said, "it's your turn."

I snapped out of my daydream, rose from the floor, and stood next to the teacher who sat in a chair. My dress was clean, my saddle shoes were polished, and my unruly hair was combed into pigtails. It was my moment. I slipped my hand into my pocket.

"I brought a balloon," I said. "Each one comes in its own wrapper." My classmates leaned forward. My teacher turned toward me for a better view. I opened the package and pulled out the balloon.

"Let me see that," my teacher said. Her hand clutched the balloon and its wrapper. She told me to sit down then called on the next student.

My face burned. At five and a half years old, I had enough sense to know I had done something wrong. But what? I wanted to ask for my balloon back, but I didn't dare.

After show and tell, I saw my teacher on the phone and heard her say my name. I was in trouble, but I didn't know why. Too embarrassed to ask her what I had done wrong, I waited for a punishment, which in my imagination grew in magnitude as the afternoon dragged on. My graham crackers and milk didn't sit well in my stomach, and naptime wasn't restful. Usually, I rode the bus home, but at the end of the day, my teacher told me my mother would pick me up. My classmates left without me.

Mom arrived shortly after the buses rolled away. The teacher invited her to sit in the chair next to her desk but told me to wait in the hallway. They would talk about me, find me guilty—of what I didn't know—and punish me forever. It had to be bad, very bad, but they didn't talk long.

"Where did you get the balloon?" Mom asked after we got in the car.

"From your dresser." Lying would've made it worse. My mother always seemed to know the answers to the questions she asked me.

"Don't go in my dresser again. Or your dad's dresser. Understand?"

I nodded in agreement. That was it. Not a word about punishment. No "wait until your father gets home." This confused me because Mom *had been called to school.* My classmates said nothing about my show-and-tell offering either, and my dreams of popularity remained buried in the playground sandbox.

Because of the eerie silence that followed my kindergarten show and tell, I never forgot about it. It wasn't until I was a freshman in high school that I realized I had taken a condom to school, and that Mom had said nothing more about the "balloon" because she didn't want to explain condoms to her five-year-old daughter.

After I figured it out, I never asked, "Hey, Mom, remember when I thought I took a balloon to kindergarten for show and tell and the teacher called you?" Like any other teenager, I didn't want to talk about birth control or sex with a parent. The *where-do-babies-come-from* talk Mom and I had when I was nine, still made me squirm with embarrassment.

After I had children, I appreciated that my kindergarten teacher and Mom handled my show-and-tell blunder with the calmness of an air traffic controller communicating with a pilot as he makes his final approach to a busy airport during a raging thunderstorm. But they never knew how much I suffered that afternoon.

Years later, I wondered if Mom might have been embarrassed because my teacher called her to school to discuss why her five-year-old daughter had a condom in her pocket. If Mom was mortified, she hid it well. She was twenty-four and had three daughters ages, five, four, and one. She may have been more horrified by the wasted condom than my taking it to school. Our family didn't have the kind of lifestyle where condoms grew on trees.

Having graduated in 1958, Mom was six years out of St. John's, a catholic high school, from which she almost didn't graduate. She had written an essay scolding the pope and the Catholic Church for banning the use of birth control by its members. If she had, instead, written an essay describing her struggles with her Catholic faith and questioning the existence of God, the nun who taught the religion class may have said, "God expects his followers will experience a crisis of faith now and then. Keep praying." But questioning the pope's stance on birth control was sacrilege.

The school threatened to withhold Mom's diploma, but she refused to rewrite her essay. She stood ready to see her high school diploma burned at the stake for the right of women to use birth control without fearing God or Hell or nuns who taught religion classes.

But Mom was also practical: She called the Wisconsin Department of Education, who made it clear to the school's administrators they could give Mom an F in religion, but they couldn't deny her a diploma because the state didn't require a religious class for graduation.

For Mom, having to talk to my kindergarten teacher about my birth-control-show-and-tell balloon was probably child's play. She had already taken on the pope *and* the Catholic Church *and* St. John's High School *and* a perturbed nun. Besides, I went to a public school, and no one threatened to keep me from graduating kindergarten.

It would be nice to know

Dror Abend-David

The Royal Academy is a good place for narcissism.
For eighteen pounds, without donation, sixteen,
you can follow Lucian Freud's self-portraits:
"This modern master of British art turns
unflinching eyes firmly on himself."
In fact, he grows more firm with time
in more ways than one.
At age twenty-seven his face is soft, blurred by doubt and remorse;
Through his thirties he paints himself into white sketches;
his features hidden by an invasive foreground
like a Madonna in a Byzantine church,
covered by the evidence of her miracles,
eyes peering as if from a Muslim headscarf.
At forty-six he is still hidden by a giant house-plant,
but among the succulent green leaves
he appears like Tarzan with torso
not unlike Johnny Weissmuller,
until seventy-one years old
he appears full frontal
painting himself a huge penis
and throughout his middle age
he grows more angular, muscular, self-assured,
in bigger frames,
and an expression of sharp determination.
Maybe it's true. Maybe he did grow more handsome,
certainly more confident.
Success could register on the face,
the hands, the muscles,
even the seventy-one-year-old penis.
The overeating that comes with professional frustration
leaves room for slender agility,
and the eyes that sag with fatigue
perk with cunning sparks.

The chest rises, the back uncoils,
feet are planted firmly on the ground.
And if not all is healed by good karma –
that is what the money is for.
Maybe nature truly works in reverse
for those who enjoy professional success.
It would be nice to know.

Time Travel in Our House

Cecil Morris

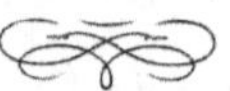

Twenty years since our daughter last glittered
in our house and twirled us to knots, and still
from time to time I find purple sparks
or silver glints in dark grout between tiles
or in hidden reaches of couch or chair
or drawer. She is everywhere eternal,
not in our memories alone, our girl
who liked to shine like a defiant star
far off even when she was home or close
in her own galaxy of secret desires
and crimes we never suspected or guessed.
For me, she is wistful and might-have-been,
a memory of mostly sweet photographs
and wild laughter, the snatch and grab of grief
now gone. For her mother, though, loss still sneaks
up and chokes out sobs—as if she were hearing
the diagnosis again, once more seeing
our daughter's demise, an ending she can't
escape—the present slips back to the past,
the past invades the future, and her loss
(eternal cavity) now echoes forth
and back: what was, what isn't, what can't be.
The errant glitter, a stray enameled
soccer pin in drawer of unlabeled keys,
her nurse's ID badge, her old scrub tops
re-purposed as quilt, all of these and more,
flux capacitors for our time machine.

Benny & Bjorn

Lilia Snowfield Anderson

Years before he ran for mayor, Benny Hansen took the ACT for his twin brother. Bjorn had always possessed a stronger knack for academics and probably would have scored better taking it himself, but he hated tests, and his brother owed him. Benny was too afraid to break up with Lana Larsen, so Bjorn had spent his Friday night dodging the slaps and screams of the head cheerleader. As Benny sat in the horridly uncomfortable folding chair in the horridly freezing gymnasium on Monday morning, he felt wildly grateful that he was doing algebra and not dealing with his girlfriend.

So Benny took the ACT twice, Bjorn broke things off with Lana, and no one was ever the wiser.

This was not unique behavior for the Hansen twins. They had learned early on that they were identical enough to replace each other in just about any situation. It started as a simple way to prank their classmates, but before long, it escalated to cheating in cross country races, getting seconds on their favorite desserts, and taking exams for one another. Neither twin was the inherent beneficiary of this system, as they split their cons fairly, each acknowledging his own skills and shortcomings and allowing the other to do the same.

By the time they were seniors in high school, the Hansen twins spent about half of each day impersonating one another. Perhaps if their mother had fewer children or their father loved them more, someone would have caught on, but no one ever did.

"They already see us as one person," Bjorn said as he tied Benny's kerchief on the night of his own eagle scout evaluation. "What does it matter if we do too? You're better at building fires anyway."

It was always assumed that the twins would go to the local community college after graduation. Their parents could afford it, there were plenty of vocations available, and they would be together. It wasn't until well into April that Bjorn mentioned doing something else.

"Let's get out of here, Benny," he said one night as they lay in their twin beds and stared at the ceiling. "Somewhere bigger than this place, somewhere we can find out who we actually are."

Benny refused to speak to his brother for almost thirty years

***

Bjorn did well in the city. He waited tables, joined a band, opened a coffee shop, and fell in love. He broke up a fight in a bar and received a scar on his cheek to show for it. Seven years after Benny stopped speaking to him, Bjorn got married. Right before the "I do's," the skies opened up and began drenching the wedding guests. The bride and groom couldn't stop laughing as they kissed in the pouring rain.

Despite all receiving invitations, not one member of the Hansen family was in attendance.

As soon as he could, Bjorn bought a car that could easily handle the four-hour drive to his hometown. His family never came to the city, but he made the trip north often. No matter how frequently he visited, how much he smiled, or how hard he made the little ones laugh, nobody ever forgave him for what he did to Benny.

"How could you just abandon him," his sister Martha hissed through her teeth as she scraped cranberry sauce from a can. It was the twenty-ninth Thanksgiving that Benny had ignored his twin brother. Bjorn had tried, as he always did, to apologize, to tell him about his life, to get anything out of the person he had shared a womb with. Martha continued as he watched Benny through the kitchen window, throwing a football with his oldest son, no trace of a smile on his face. "He needed you, and you left him."

"I asked him to come with me," Bjorn said to his sister, his eyes unmoving from the scene in the barren November backyard. They had this conversation multiple times a year, and Bjorn knew the lines that came next. *Are you too good for this town? Too good for us? Benny needed you. He was so sad when you left.* His sister spoke and he let her, her words a variation of the script he had heard his entire adulthood, her voice fading into the background as he stared out the window.

***

On the ride home from Thanksgiving with the Hansens, Lana finally told Benny what had been bothering her for months.

"If we don't do something soon, we will lose all our progress."

She was referring to, of course, the status she had worked tirelessly to build. Since their dating days, Lana had known Benny was a good horse to hitch her wagon to. He was from one of the oldest families in town, had been a good athlete in high school, and had stuck around when his twin hadn't. He also taught ninth-grade geography, meaning every parent in town had to, at the very least, respect him.

Despite all of this, Lana needed more. "You need to run for mayor," she said simply.

Her husband, miles away in his own thoughts, turned toward her. "What?" he asked before hitting a pothole and nearly swerving off the road.

"It will be good for us," she said, turning to ensure the kids were still asleep. "You know Andrew isn't going to be as good of an athlete as you were, and I don't think Lydia will be all that pretty. This could help them."

Benny was too shocked to anger at his wife's comments about their children. She continued. "Mayor is the most powerful position in town. We'd get the best seats at church, maybe some discounts on groceries. And nobody on the PTA will ever try and steamroll my Spring Fling ideas again. Don't you want that?"

While Benny wanted to say no, to yell at his wife, to pull the car over and make her walk home, nothing came out of his mouth. The memory of taking the ACT twice, so he didn't have to confront Lana flooded his mind. He had aged, but Benny Hansen still lacked the courage to stand up to this woman. How he wished Bjorn was here now.

But, just as he had been for the past twenty-nine years, Benny was alone. He sighed.

"Sure, honey. I'll run for mayor."

***

The day after Thanksgiving, after Martha came to take the kids sledding and Lana left to shop, Benny poured a fresh thermos of coffee and started driving toward the city. He had four hours to figure out how he would handle everything. It felt wrong, he noted, to be going about things this way, as if all the anger, resentment, and pain of his adulthood were being washed away for the sake of his wife's popularity.

He was wondering why he ever married Lana – and how he probably wouldn't have if Bjorn had stuck around – when he saw his twin brother pulled over on the side of the highway. He parked his car, which Lana had insisted he get in black, behind Bjorn's gray Subaru. His feet felt heavy against the pavement as he walked toward his brother.

"I'm fine," Bjorn huffed as he wrenched the tire jack. "Just gotta get this.

Benny stood silently as Bjorn stared into his own face, eyes wide and mouth agape.

Later, after the tire had been changed, a bar had been entered, and seven beers had been drunk, Benny told Bjorn what he could do to make up for leaving.

Current mayor Jerry Meyer had surprised no one when he resigned at the Monday evening city council meeting, confirming what everyone already knew – there would be a special election to replace him. The scandal surrounding Mr. Meyer was significant enough that stepping down was his only option. He had received four DUIs in three months, the final arrest having been made by his wife. She had been on duty when she saw her husband and his nineteen-year-old girlfriend swerving wildly and tossing condoms out the window.

Benny's campaign was announced the following Friday afternoon in his homeroom period. It was a strategic and calculated plan he had no part in crafting. His students cheered and immediately began designing posters and suggesting campaign songs. Other than Lana in the back of the classroom, recording the entire event and preparing to upload it later that evening, it was a sweet and private moment.

The other candidates presented themselves the following week. Mike Baxter, president of the local VFW post, announced his candidacy at the Tuesday potluck. Nobody had seen him smile in eighteen years, but he almost let one loose when he saw the sheet cake that read "Mike for Mayor!" in thick, buttercream frosting.

Valerie Vernon, a former student of Benny's, posted a polished, professional, and purposeful announcement from outside her office at the social service building. Her bubbly personality and comprehensive platform pushed her video to state news outlets, but even she knew she was too young and too liberal for a town like this.

If it weren't for Willow Jean Barkley, Benny Hansen would have won the mayoral election without even trying. His family was well known, he wasn't linked to any scandals, and his politics were benign enough. But Widow Willow, as Lana referred to her, had lost her reverend husband in a hunting accident a few years prior. She was also the only realtor in a forty-mile radius. Everyone needed her, whether they were attempting to sell their single-wide or upgrade to a lakefront property.

There was no way Benny Hansen could beat Willow Jean Barkley.

***

Lana followed Benny, her phone always recording, to every campaign event, posting what looked good and deleting what didn't. She was always amazed how he found time to update the website, help Andrew and Lydia with their homework, and grade his students' papers. "It's like you're in two places at once!" she'd say as she stared at her husband.

Two weeks after he announced his candidacy, Benny was endorsed by the teacher's union. The nurses association, electricians guild, and service workers federation quickly followed. He posed for the front page of the paper, a Santa hat hanging off his head and a Salvation Army bell in his hand. Lana posted a video of him delivering gifts at the nursing home that got over 50,000 views. "Nothing like that deadbeat brother of his," one comment read.

Lana found herself actually wanting to have sex with her husband. She pursued him constantly, at night and in the morning, her desire only growing stronger the more ground Benny gained in the polls. He wasn't always game, however, and often pushed her aside, telling her it wasn't a good time.

Lana wasn't the only one newly captivated by Benny Hansen. Articles in the paper spoke of his charisma and charm, two words that had never been used to describe him before.

"I don't know what it is, but I'm much more likely to buy your brother a beer now than I was before he started running," Martha Hansen's husband said, his mouth full of hamburger hotdish. It was election night, and Benny was neck and neck with Willow Jean Barkley. The local news, glowing from Martha's tiny kitchen TV, played a clip of the two candidates shaking hands at last week's VA pancake breakfast. "He looks like he's been working out, doesn't he, Mar?" her husband asked. Martha didn't respond, her eyes fixed on the screen as she wondered if Benny had always had that little scar on his cheek.

***

Mr. Hansen found out he had beaten Willow Jean Barkley in a conference room at the Holiday Inn. His campaign team and family surrounded him, silent and shaking as he took the call from Jerry Meyer.

"Thank you, Mr. Mayor," he said with a chuckle before hanging up and fist-pumping the air. Everyone cheered. His father shook his hand, his mother cried, and Lana kissed him in public for the first time since their wedding day. After thanking everyone, the new mayor politely excused himself, saying he needed a bit of air.

He left the hotel and walked across the parking lot with a smile on his face. Glancing over his shoulder to ensure nobody was following him, he slid into the driver's seat of a gray Subaru.

"We did it, Benny," he exhaled.

His brother glanced up from the papers he was grading in the passenger seat. His eyes scanned Bjorn's face, his own face, before moving down to the shirt he had chosen for the occasion. Blue and checkered, it was crisp and professional but not too flashy for a small town. Benny was wearing the same one. He undid the top two buttons to match his twin.

"I was thinking," Bjorn said, the smile unmoving from his face, "You, Lana, and the kids should come to the city next week. "Teresa and I would love to make you lunch and show you around. You could spend the night, as long as you don't mind a Saint Bernard licking your face in the morning," he laughed.

Benny straightened his papers, refusing to meet his brother's eye. "It's great I won," he said. A moment of silence followed as the smile slowly melted off Bjorn's face. Without another word, Benny left the car and started walking toward the hotel.

Despite the whirlwind that was the mayoral campaign, the rest of election night would be remembered as severely underwhelming. The charismatic Benny seemingly disappeared into thin air after he won. His acceptance speech was dull, full of stuttering, and went on far too long. The celebration festivities Lana had planned were over before they'd even begun.

After, former mayor Jerry Meyer would insist that he drove by the Holiday Inn and saw two Benny Hansens in the parking lot. "One had his head out the car, crying like a baby and yelling at the other one," he would say when he told the story.

Nobody believed former mayor Jerry Meyer, of course.

NEWS

J. Nishida

Thoughts Travelling Louder than a Car Racing on the Midnight Street

Jiewei Li (李劼韦)

A weird dimension in a muffled rain-scented hotel with red carpet:
"If the hallway of a hotel leads like a labyrinth,
it will trap lost souls."

HIM:
"If you really want to please me,
kiss me on my temples.
(My temples with trees and ponds and amphibians)."

PTSD:
"If the birds suddenly align themselves in the sky,
it takes me back to the days in a red-foxhole."

Me:
"If this is my life,
I'd rather not grow old.
(I won't regret not seeing the amber sunset of my life)."

The taxi driver:
"If the temperature continues to drop like this,
I will call global warming a hoax.
(It's burning hot, it's burning red)."

Imagery from a hot summer:
The toad emerged fresh out of a pond,
only to be squashed by a rushing vehicle.
(and he ended up in a red pool).

*Then he said I told you, I'm not well, you know,
I just bleed, it's not a big deal."*

The taxi stopped in the middle of the street (so did my mind),
where the night has disenchanted the charm of the red and green.
They still work on a different realm though:
the rain, the wind, the ones in love and the dead roaming the lonely roads,
in midair, in memory, in desperation and in hopes.

No, Doctor, Come to Me
Not to be Cured

Lawrence Bridges

This reach believes newly greened lives
should grasp elevators before high-rise iron
skeletons them with trailer parks
and protest banners, while rides wait with no
summoning on the avenues below.
I'm flattened by bodies falling in playboy mode
who found plenty to do before detecting
an edge where shafts, repellent to intoxicants
and further hovering for sport, desisted
with a winding-down fan. Oh, jumpsuit
and helmet, you invite such stares
on conformity powered streets,
where everyone's left guessing until a pick
to celebrate emerges – then styles change.
It started in lobbies where you lived vertically,
removed from dirty green things,
beside the intake vent.

Chiaroscuro Desolato

Greg Bell

Golden light, or is it   amber light
Shelters me from burning of the sun
How delightful is this golden light!

With petals of the rose once fragrant, bright
I wake to find my pillow overrun
In golden light,   or is it   amber light?

Tired rose, tired petals in the dun alight
I rise to see the sky with smoke is hung
How delightful was this golden light.

Ten thousand acres burning to affright
Ten million people trembling, undone
Golden light, or writhing amber light –

Five hundred thousand acres charred to blight
Ninety thousand flee their homes, on the run
But yet   delightful was this golden light –

With endless desolation, loss of life
Apocalypse in Paradise has spun
Golden light, or writhing amber night
How dire   this golden light

There's No Way Back Home to Mariupol: Sashko's Story of Survival

Taras Bereza

4:30 a.m. February 24. The first few bombs from above marked the lightning attack across the country, from east to west. A few turbulent minutes shook everyone's peace and comfort forever. The new normal came with the scenes of devastation, helpless elderly, mothers with crying children hugged tough, and abandoned pets on the streets. With minimum belongings, people hid in shelters waiting for another bomb to be dropped.

Weeks before, we were all busy in the routines of daily life, dreamt wild, built plans, raised children, earned a living, and sought happiness as far as it was possible. Normally, we complained about high household fees and blamed bad politicians for lack of reforms, low salaries, and Covid-19, let alone poorly repaired roads. Life went on as usual until the sky fell over Ukraine.

On the 86th day of the devastating warfare here, every single soul has lost much. The scenes of bombarded cities sinking in debris and rubble make a nightmarish story to share with the rest of the world. One hundred forty-six children killed and hundreds forcefully deported to the Russian-occupied territories is no excuse at all. The red line was crossed long ago with 10 million refugees bound to leave their homes. On the once beautifully decorated streets of Mariupol, rambling cats and dogs are now wandering around the emptied streets for anything edible left on the spot.

My hometown Lviv, in the deep west of Ukraine, has been lucky to appear backstage on the battlefield (not counting several rocket bombs we have received from the Russians.) That's indeed nothing compared to the almost smashed cities of Mariupol, Kharkiv, and Chernihiv. We are on a mission to help thousands of temporarily re-settled refugees with food and shelter.

My guest these days is Ihor from Mariupol. It took him five enduring days to cross the distance of more than 1000 miles and reach Lviv. This 61-year-old former officer of the Soviet army was urged to revive his stamina and wit to transport his wife, mother-in-law, and a just-adopted son, Sashko. Sashko's mother was buried in rubble with 300 others at the Mariupol Drama Theater. Ihor and Olena fetched him to safety and without a second thought, they decided to adopt the kid.

Through the blackness of night, they tried to move across the bumpy roads near the fields and woods not to be caught or killed. "The vaguer the whereabouts, the better, just not to get spotted by the Russians," Ihor confessed. Humiliating encounters with the Russian separatists on the roadblocks were inevitable, though. During one of the occasions, Olena told Russians that their family was all 'Covid-infected' and warned them not to get closer. Fully equipped with medical kinds of stuff, they used Sashko as their tactical shield. A wounded patient with a high temperature who urgently needed hospitalization – such was their hard-luck story to wit out the Russian guards. Eventually, all these tricks worked well and helped my future guests get to Lviv safe and sound.

I have never seen Ihor before. We got close on the phone due to his membership in my online Language Club. His late afternoon call on Sunday came as a sheer surprise to me. After 11 days of disappearance in Mariupol, he phoned me from Market Square in the city's downtown. I immediately agreed to share shelter with them.

The first thing I spotted while hugging Ihor as an old pal was a beam of optimism in his eyes. The immediate touch turned my perception of the war's kaleidoscope upside down. With thousands of those killed and wounded, broken destinies on the ruins of ghost cities, Ihor reflected a perpetual zest for life.

With a moral compass of such a caliber, I am yet to re-consider a whole sense of life while still miles away from the battleground. Instead of grief over the whole drama of war filled with atrocities and dire straits, I saw a surge of life in his eyes. With no possible return to Mariupol, the family is heading for France soon.

Ihor acquainted me with his newly adopted son, Sashko. An overwhelmingly energetic 12-year-old child who smiled at me. He's a lucky one to have survived the bombardment beneath the Drama Theatre, I thought. In my house, the howl of wind did not take him unawares. Bound to sleep as far from the window as possible, Sashko could not count the stars that night. Nonetheless, he believed in the power of dreams. That was perhaps the only thing nobody would ever take away from him. Coming from an underclass family with a despotic father and mother toiling on the docks, Sashko had to survive in the daytime and dream about better days at night. Our 'treasure on the road,' as Ihor and Olena now call him. Ihor's shining diamond after he lost his first son when Russians invaded Ukraine in 2014 for the first time.

As a father of three, I would compare Sashko to Oliver Twist, a lucky survivor of a major life challenge. On the brink of death, Sashko somehow appeared in the right place the moment when the building was hit by the half-ton bomb. He is now up to a new high in the ebb and flows of his new life. His new destination, whatever it is, entails no point of return. Through the new destinations and challenges, he is bound to survive the future ahead. Still, it is nothing else but a sheer blessing with a second chance in life. I much hope that Sashko will value this lifetime opportunity and always cherish the deed of his new parents.

One day, I believe, he will return to his motherland and show the re-built hometown to his wife and children. The moment of truth will come through timeworn recollections of his dramatic survival towards a new life. At least, he would predict a better future, to honor *Mariupol* as the ghost city of his treacherous childhood.

jealousy case study 1

Deviant Bates

before evelyn's   smile
  I pronounced   ecstasy
    like a sad walk home

for instance one
   boy
    shuddered
  his spirit
   loose
     as stars

   in evelyn's eyes
   this is my first
   tough pill

     I did skin the big dipper
  first   by mistake
  and evelyn
called
  me

bad at polyamory

Could This be Some Kind of Koan?
Peggy Landsman

(Upon informing one of my professors that I will not be pursuing graduate
studies in his department…)

"What do you
expect to accomplish,"
he asks, "by the time
you're thirty?"

"Nothing," I say,
and think to myself,
but why stop
at thirty?

The Piano Teacher

Sydney Sinks

17. She told me about a story she saw on the news. A family had painted their entire house blue. Blue paneling, streaks of teal dripping down window frames and bleeding into indigo, shutters coated with cerulean brushstrokes. And over the blue, they added swirls of gold and white. The night sky, pockmarked with stars.

"They painted *Starry Night* all over their house," she explained.

I smiled at the sheet music and tried to picture it. This song, titled after Van Gogh's painting, was meant to capture its essence in music. Synesthesia on the page. As she described the painting, I gave a note to each star—that C belonged to a gold star, the A belonged to a blazing white one. Each crescendo was a shower of comets.

"Play it again," she said.

She closed her eyes to listen. I began carefully, brushing each key so that the pressure and sound were even, not one star shining brighter than the others. Gentle, sleeping, then louder and demanding, the heavy black tree in the corner of the painting, *see me*. Triplets dribbled down the staff, a smattering of constellations.

"For the love of God," she said when I was finished, "practice with a metronome."

***

14. I slouched behind her, trying not to get too close. She adjusted the bench's height and curled her wrists over the keys. "Can you see?" she asked pointedly, and I took a reluctant step closer. I was afraid to crowd her.

"When you press down hard," she said, and demonstrated, "it gets louder. But lightly—and—more quiet. Weighted keys."

My face flushed. I nodded furiously, embarrassed that I didn't already know this basic fact about pianos. *I should know more.* "That's cool," I said, then immediately berated myself for not saying something more profound.

"And this is how this will sound. Count it when you play. One and two and three and four and." As she spoke, she played a basic melody. "Try it."

I slid onto the bench as she stood up. My fingers fumbled over the keys. I couldn't remember which one was C. We both stared at my hands for several seconds as I struggled to control them.

"You'll get the hang of it," she decided.

That night, I dragged the keyboard from my room to the innermost concrete corner of our basement where no one would be able to hear. I practiced the same lines for hours until finally my hands started to obey.

***

16. My fingers drummed a two-octave scale against my thigh. Nervous habit. I sat on the sagging steps of the building, stomach twisted, and waited. Three weeks after getting my license, the third time driving to the lesson on my own, and the car wouldn't start. I gulped at the winter air, trying to push back panicked tears brimming in my eyes.

The door opened behind me. A short intake of breath. Startled. "Oh, hello," she said automatically. Sheet music slid out of her arms and blew down the steps. I jumped onto my knees and swept the pages into a haphazard pile, muttering my apology.

"Did you need something?" she asked. The lesson ended twenty minutes ago. Her gnarled fingers clutched at the buttons of her coat as she pulled it tighter around her.

"No. Sorry. I'm just waiting for my dad to pick me up."

Her eyes flicked to my car.

"It won't start."

"Oh." We stared at each other for a minute. I opened my mouth to apologize again, but she spoke first. "Well, come inside. It's cold out here."

"You don't have to—" I started, but the door was already closing behind her. I caught it and followed.

***

16. "Like singing. You start loud, with a big breath. But what happens at the end of the lyric?"

I stared at the sheet music, searching for an answer. "You...trail off? Sort of?"

"Yes, exactly. You get quieter. *Cantabile.* Play it like you'd sing it. When you're practicing, sing it out loud sometime and hear when you get quiet."

"Okay, so kind of like this?" I took a deep breath, slowly, and leaned my weight into the keys, then lessened the pressure until it was almost silent, the music growing fainter as my lungs constricted. The harmony stayed consistent, quiet but there.

"Yes, just like that. Even more. Start louder. You don't play loudly enough. Sometime when no one's home, play as loud as you can. Just let go and shake the house." She leaned back in her chair and studied me. "You're too quiet. I was quiet once, too. But not anymore."

I suddenly saw her as she was growing up in the 40s, a young girl in a world that frowned on loud women. A blaze of connection between us. I dropped my hands back to my lap and stretched my fingers.

"I wish I wasn't so quiet," I admitted, then blushed.

"Hmm. Well, there's nothing wrong with it. Some people just like to hear themselves talk and that's no good either," she said. "You should play louder, though. And try being louder. You have good things to say." Then, like an afterthought, "My daughter is quiet."

She shuffled the music books together and I stood, understanding that as my cue. "Do you see her a lot?" Immediate fear that I might have over-stepped. I stared at the floor.

"She lives in Milwaukee. She'll come home for Thanksgiving."

My eyes flicked to the wedding ring that was too big; it always twisted around her swollen knuckle when she played so that the diamond scraped the keys. She never mentioned him. Did she live alone in her big house? Did any-one check on her during the week?

"That will be fun." I inched toward the door. I didn't want to go, but I was never sure if I overstayed my welcome. Sometimes at night when the world was finally quiet, I imagined what it would be like to stay in this creak-ing building all week. I could hide away here and be a fly on the wall, watch the parade of teachers and students, hear the strains of violin music filter down the stairs, rest my head on the doorframe and listen to the aching voice of the piano.

She smiled at me. "Yup. See you next week."

***

15. I stood outside the closed door and listened. It was beautiful. Arpeggios stumbled down the keys. A crescendo swelled to fill the hallway and then shat-tered into tinkling eighth notes. The pedal creaked, notes glued together and melded and reverberated. I was paralyzed, listening to her play. With every gentle note, I breathed. With every forceful pounding of the keys, my eyelids fluttered, and I smiled. It was safe here. An oasis in this building once a week.

The music slowed and stopped.

I raised a reluctant fist to the door and knocked.

***

18. Outside, the sun was shining and the temperature had crawled up to eighty for the first time that year, but my bare arms prickled in the artificial cold of the lobby. I shuffled my music as a way to occupy my hands, telling myself to stay relaxed. All too well, I remembered being fourteen and pacing the lobby.

She beelined toward me, anxious to ask how the audition went, what the judge said, if I was pleased.

"Let's sit. We'll get your results in a minute," she said. I nodded. This was the fourth year in a row, the last time that I would stay up until 3 a.m. practicing, the last time before I left for college. The last time. Graduation was tomorrow. I breathed and stretched my fingers, relieved that it was over, already painfully nostalgic.

"I think the *Starry Night* was okay," I told her.

"Did you trip over the triplets?"

"Not this time."

"Then I'm sure it was better than okay," she said, and I smiled.

We stared at the floor. I sat beside her and bounced my knee. I tasted what I wanted to say but swallowed the words.

Instead, I fumbled in my bag, pulled out a blue envelope, and pressed it into her hands. I don't always know how to say what I mean, but I can write. I had to write it all down so she would know.

She tucked the letter into her purse, promising to read it later, and smiled at me. "We had a good long run, you and I," she said, and I nodded. Four years, all through high school. Now I was gone, moving across the state.

"You leave for school in August?"

"Yup."

"Stop by before you go. Keep in touch," she said, and when she looked at me, I knew she meant it. I promised I would. I thought of the letters I would write her in my dorm room, the easygoing visit I would pay at Thanksgiving, the quiet things we would talk about when we met again.

I knew that this was my last audition. I wish that I had known then about a different, bigger last.

Later, when we hugged, I held my breath as I folded my arms around her. She walked me to the door.

"Good luck," she called suddenly. I turned. She was smiling, excited for me. "Enjoy every minute of it. I know I did."

I clutched at her parting words of advice, her final lesson, and nodded at the old woman. Then I pushed open the heavy glass doors and let them close behind me. We waved goodbye. The summer air pulled me forward.

Taiwo Hassan

forgive me, deep blue sea

for my great-grandmother and my grandmother and my
mother,   and their feathery *iboruns*, the ones that wear subtle shades of your
essence, washed tough and rinsed hard - like their bodies at your bank, immersed
in elements dense enough to make darkness cower yet tender, despite, light
enough to make a zephyr jealous.

forgive me, deep blue sea,
for their colorful *ipèlés*, passed down, adorned in tears, smiles and camphor,
balancing soothing weights of history in their neat creases and heavy stories in
their countless beads,
edges elastic enough to tuck in kinky braids of jet black hair till they meet their
grey siblings yet heavy enough to be another noun for dignity, to honor my sisters,
and their daughters.

forgive me, deep blue sea,
for this man, this found wanderer, this box of metaphors
rethinking himself your vastness, hoping he could also stretch enough to flow into
poems and fill empty stanzas with nostalgia while thickening thin lines with
words of their past.
you must have heard whispers around what they say about heads washed at your
intersections, about where the seeds of cut hair go to grow, where they go to
morph into trees, into grace.

forgive me, deep blue sea,
for the countless heartbreaks i've painted with your fleeting foams, and the shards
of their broken silences that double as ironies found only in the melodies of your
waves.   for this poem, for the little ways i've tried to measure your saltiness and
how i still fail to carry that scale well.   for the ways i've designed grief in your
name, how i've confused its vastness with yours, for the countless times i've
numbed myself enough to think i hold what you do, thinking myself a similar body,
just in a deeper shade of blue.

forgive me, deep blue sea.

iborùn - scarf in Yorùbá language
ìpèlé - a special type of women's clothing in Yorùbá language

the dawn strayed to the mouth of the forest, we caught it singing with a tongue of stone

(erasure [text from the song of enchantments; Ben Okri, chapter 9; half miracles]

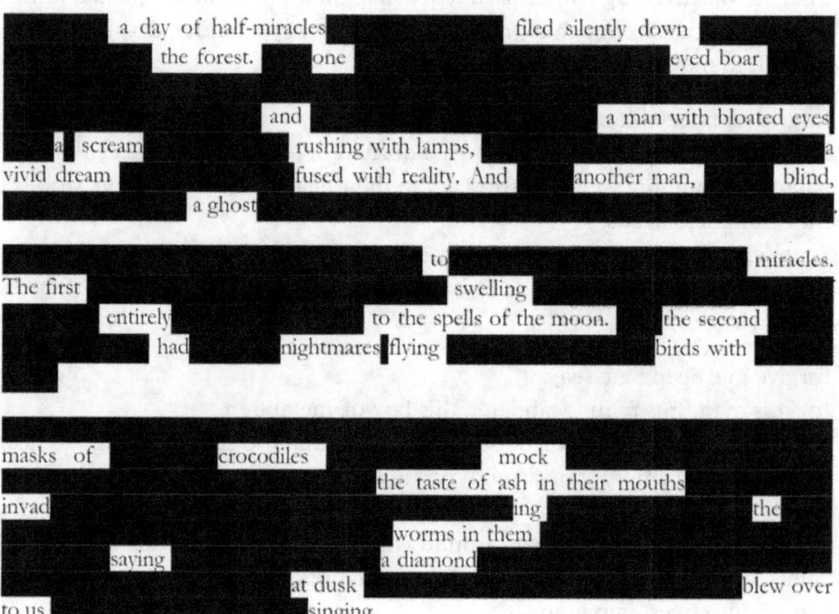

The Dawn Strayed
Olumide Manuel

Off Marvin Key

Ann Weil

A capsized boat, sunset gleaming
over its gray curved hull.
Red lights lit, police boats hovered,
rocked in the rising swells.

From shore we thought we understood,
hoped those aboard could swim,
turned our backs to the drama, walked
away under the palms.

Next day, we learned that eyes deceive,
that nature takes what she
wants. No sunken boat, but a whale
beached dead off Marvin Key.

Forty-seven feet long and gaunt,
his wrecked body suffered
disease or virus, we supposed.
Not one of us offered

the truth autopsy would reveal.
Intestines strangled, sick
with our ignorant obsession—
plastic, plastic, plastic.

Girl Sunsplit

Neethu Krishnan

A temple procession circles the perimeter. Drums and bells, firecrackers in the pauses. It's mid-April. Around ten in the morning. I'm cross-legged on my bed, the AC safeguarding me from the talons of South Indian heat. Padding to the dark-tinted, curtained windows of my bedroom, I keen my ear to the thuds and clangs, trying to gauge how long till they snail to the road facing the front of our house.

A quick peek from the porch, that's all I plan on, nothing more.

The echoes sound hours away.

Even through the night-like glass, the sun looks furious, making me brim with gratitude for the month-old ivory machine whirring above me.

Click. Wheeze. Click.

The AC shudders its mouth shut, the ceiling fan following suit—no longer a blurred circle, but three gyrating blades chopping to a slow death.

***

Our station is only minutes away. Despite the train's panting speed, each second only seems to stretch longer than the last. We are queued in the corridor: my impatient dad at the front, herding more baggage than anyone should at an open, rattling train door, my little brother and I, our rucksacks half-emptied of the mountain of snacks and candy we boarded with, and mum—a childish smile butterflying across her round face—with a jute carry-bag, the containers in its belly emptied of breakfast, idlis and tomato chutney. Peering through the nearest horizontal-grated windows, we count down familiar landmarks until our two-minute halt, which when it beams into view, finally— thick black paint strokes of *Kayamkulam* spelled out in English, Hindi and Malayalam against school-bus yellow—untwists geysers of anticipatory joy through our file.

Ribbons of humid heat garland around us. Though baked and matted with soot and peak summer for two days in the open-windowed-yet-stuffed sleeper train, the sun refracting off the clean air and the deluge of greens is a welcome kiss. Once an autorickshaw or a white Ambassador taxi delivers us to one of my parents' homes, time accordions.

A satisfying black stream rivers against white ceramic as I scrub myself clean of the train, but before it can run transparent, it's the morning of the return journey for us tanned, plump kids to our homes and schools in Mumbai.

***

The walls and bedsheets cling to a faint signature of the last puffs of the AC. It's a daytime power cut even though there's no hint of rain. The power lines seem at the mercy of the monsoon breeze; even the gentlest stir cuts out the power, or the operators do, prophylactically. But the sky is blazing, no grays smudge the horizon, and yet.

I'm drawing composed breaths, trying not to exhaust the last vestiges of cold cupped in my bedroom. I'm praying the load-shedding be the accidental kind, the reinstated-within-an-hour kind. Another half hour is the farthest I can elasticize the calm before I disintegrate.

***

The radio hums old Malayalam tunes. Grandmother hums along. The kitchen exhales dove-gray clouds from its rectangle mouth—a cutout in the tarry wall behind the firewood stove, a short adult's height from the floor—into the canvas sky. The bulk of the exhaust twirls through the house, heavy shafts of it perfusing the grandparents' bedroom, temporarily ours for the vacation—the only room with a fan.

Above the ebony wood ceiling from which dangles the fan, nail-clicking critters, rat-to-cat sized, can be heard zooming about, dislodging soot and antiquated spider web lumps, also onyx, from the panel joints onto the bed, sometimes, straight into our saucer eyes. We rarely lounge inside the house when there's honeyed paradise outside, but if we do, my brother and I run the fan only at its lowest speed, or not at all, lest the black-furred ochre contraption draws the whole roof down with it, terracotta tiles, mystery creatures and all, snapping the precarious wiring securing the ancient brittle in place.

We lunch with lights on, radio humming in the background, in the smoke-painted bedroom where even the lizards are tuxedoed black.

At the threshold of the house, framed by the kingfisher-blue door, grandfather gets ready for bath, brownish-black particles of crisp-fried onion and curry leaves in the coconut oil crunching between his spade-like palms as he rubs them together before massaging it on his balding-at-places shiny scalp, gray tufts of hair spiking and glistening with the fragrant oil.

The radio hushes. The tube light flickers off. Grandfather mumbles mild annoyance at the power cut. We chuckle. The radio is his white noise, an everyday ritual. Once switched on at eleven in the morning, he goes off into the fields. At two, when the radio automatically switches relay to Delhi and the language from Malayalam, the only one he understands, to Hindi, he materializes out of seemingly nowhere, dashes to turn it off and disappears out again.

Steel plates loaded with rice and curry in hand, we emerge from the dark cave of the bedroom into the corridor, where there's no dearth of sun. Large sections of the outside-facing walls are criss-crosses of vibrant, kingfisher blue painted wood, just like the twin front doors and their frames. Seating ourselves on the narrow bench and desk in the corridor, we finish our meals, large diamonds of warm light tickling our sweaty backs.

***

I've lost count of the hours since the power outage. I assume it's lunchtime from mum's busyness. She pops in hourly from the kitchen to check on me. The last time she came in, throwing open the curtains, the windows and the bedroom door, she assured me the natural breeze from the tree groves hugging the house was just as good, that I'll be okay.

Lying flat on my bed, head propped up by pillows, my bones are liquid, the room spinning around me. An unmoving rock obstructs my throat—doesn't slide down, doesn't dislodge up and out. Shrapnel inside my wrists. I've left them undisturbed, limp, flattened out against the mattress, and yet the electric pain corkscrews up my arms. My head is mush, its insides sloshing violent with the slightest movement. Blinks are too disorienting. Open eyes are worse. The spinning room weighs like lead on my sockets. I want to pluck them out, freeze the room motionless.

Sweat spiders all over. I itch to wrench off my clothes, skin, body.

***

Our pudgy, browning-deeper-by-the-minute hands dig into the toasty, gold sand, feathering it from one velveted palm to another. The noon casts dwarf shadows of me and my brother on our sand kingdoms. Furnished with waterways, bedrooms, halls, and towers that serve no purpose but to hoist triangle flags, its kitchenettes bursting with faux condiments plucked from the acreage of weeds and shrubs and its treasure chests housing an ultramarine marble, a pinky-sized sickle, a walnut-sized blue plastic pearl and a fistful of lustrous lucky red seeds, our sandcastles are elaborate enough constructions to mimic a poorly planned township forced into a single unit of architecture.

We sneak cold water from the easy-to-access bucketfuls of it on the raised concrete platform of the well—drawn and filled into aluminium buckets by grandmother for her afternoon stone-wash laundry and grandfather for his bath—but our paper boats still sink to the shallow, finger-indented canal floor of our sandy waterways. No matter how many mugfuls we pour in, the peevish sun sucks it dry with an invisible straw before our very eyes, competing with which, we keep refilling them, in vain, till sundown; our energies infinite, inexhaustible, until darkness dapples our kingdom and mum summons us inside.

Grandmother sweeps, with her stick broom, concentric arcs around the house, including the backyard where our magnificent civilizations are, and my brother and I can't wait patiently enough for the first light next day to redo a new blueprint for our broom-attacked, flattened and now traceless city, hopefully aiming for a parch-proof settlement in the soft, malleable lap of inviting, feathery alluvium.

***

It's four in the evening. Hot streaks race to my ears. The rock chokes any sound that threatens to escape my throat. I'm a husk in the furnace of my room. Lemon juice, water, water with instant glucose: mum's attempts to compensate for the leak of water, energy, hope. She asks me to stop crying, it'll only make it worse. I'm aware the tears are pointless, but they are not deliberate, conscious. I don't possess the energy to invoke words. I can't nod or shake my head in protest either, the world is already a carousel, nauseating me to helpless tears. Flicking my pinky finger, as much as it can budge against the quiver, I gesture assent or otherwise to mum's queries.

Grandmother waddles in once or twice, gently stroking my wrists and legs, trying to pray my pain away each time. Even frail grandfather shuffles in, supported by grandmother's steadying clasp, braving the slippery white Marbonite tiles to check in on his sick granddaughter, causing my chest to flutter with anger and sadness for my poor grandparents.

I should be the one hovering and caring. This upside-down version where I add to their worries is infuriating.

The lava roiling under my forehead fumes and froths, torches me from the inside, reminds me the limits of my voluntary control over my own body.

This isn't what it used to be like.

Resentment mingles with waters of frustration, tracks salt-bedded, undrying trails on my cheeks.

***

My cerulean cotton skirt, sequinned with holographic silver, flashes like a disco ball the morning of the house-warming ceremony. Each fingertip-sized circle fractures the sun into a kaleidoscope of colours, broadcasting a web of dancing brilliance around me—on the whites of the old soil and on the new house's flooring of milky Marbonite. I swish and pirouette, the sun sieved to a carpet of mesmerizing stars trailing and haloing me.

The old house with the blue criss-crosses and smoked interiors bustles with guests ten strides to the right of our new two-story house. I shuttle to and fro, bypassing the umbrella of the sprawling cashew tree between the two, capering only in swathes of unhindered sun to skitter florets of rainbow luminescence on my path like a benediction.

I'm invincible, ethereal; chipping the gilded sun to confetti, a million iridescent coins spring forth from me.

***

The procession still sounds far away. Or it has passed and the cymbals resound in my head. I remember the punches of unbearable sound twitching the air, pummelling my ears, splintering my attempts of forced sleep for so long, it felt like there wasn't a before, won't be an after, without the reverberating percussive thunders.

I'm in the mint green bathroom. Steadied by mum's arms, one hooked around me, the other gripping my drooping arm, I toddled till the sand-coloured fibre door. She helped me in, closed the door, asked me to keep it unlatched lest I collapse inside like the first time all this erupted and silted permanent—the day we returned to our Mumbai home after my junior college vacations; the year one couldn't tell the bed and me apart; the beginning of the after. The life of heat fearing, cold worshipping, sun hating, any trace of heat slow-poisoning me thence to a puddle of helplessly nauseated, head-spinning meat.

Propped up against the cool mint walls, I pour plastic cup after trembling cup of insipid water on me like an offering to a stone deity. I keep at it until the buckets filled in the morning empty; the sun melts into the raven tank on the terrace, so I don't open the taps for a refill. I towel gingerly, a fleeting, protective film of water left on as I clothe. I'd crawl back to bed if I could move my head without the earth shifting violent, but, of course, I can't, so, mum helps me upright, steers me back to the bedroom.

The fronds of light wane. The fan—bone yellow—hangs useless. The operators inform us of the fallen tree that damaged the power lines on its earthbound swing. The repairs necessitate a timeframe definitely longer than a day.

Mum swings to action the moment the holy light of the AC glows on and the fan resuscitates the next evening, shutting the windows, curtaining them, closing my bedroom door and assuring me everything'll be better in no time.

I'm flopped in bed: disorientated, molten, a nebula of spinning molecules. Gratitude is a wispy quiver through the idea of me; I've run the tear ducts dry.

A surge of cold cocoons me. Relieved, I nestle into the dryness. I keep my eyes trained on the muted sun, nose-pressed against my window, as the cold kneads its chilly fingers into me, reconstituting me from an infinite incoherence of molecules into a finite and mostly non-ionized human-approximating whole.

The Nighttime Car

Julie McNeely-Kirwan

I hear the breathing of machines
and suddenly it is my
hands that I see.

They're on a steering wheel
in a ten-and-two death grip,
behind crap headlights
throwing out a field of vision
in glorious black and white,
carried constantly ahead.
I am traveling fast, running past
Joshua trees and
the endless possibility
of fine monsters
on either half-lit side.
Glowing and broken,
yellow lines
show the way,
gravel-strewn asphalt
slides beneath the car,
giving it purchase.
There isn't much moon,
but by now the dark hides
only the shy beasts
who were mine
all along.

I am driving,
snug in the nighttime car,
with its slow AC and
faux leather seats,
with its ticky-tack heater and
and roll-up windows,
with its gifts of music and

cool water and a backpack
that might contain anything.

On the stony verge,
a fox shows herself
for a moment
then slips back
into the beautiful dark,
to more Joshua trees
and hill cities of rock.

For I am driving
the nighttime car,
and might see
any miracle.

The nurse returns with
slim hypodermics and
appropriate empathy.
One can barely hear the
breathing of the machines.
My blood waits.

But I am already well
away from empty rooms
and doors left ajar,
from closed accounts
and notices of sale.
My gewgaws are
gone, given, hurled, and
my might-have lives,
once hidden and hoarded,
are disintegrating prettily
in a yard somewhere,
like stage-painted cardboard.

I am traveling light,
am on my way.
I am driving the nighttime car.

Song of Title

Piper Samuels

Piper was a beach bird.
Piper's friends were shore fishes, everyone.
Piper was a fish and a bird and a girl and a Ponyo.
Piper's hair was messy and sandy and tangled and Piper didn't notice and
Piper thought the ocean smelled so salty and
Piper loved the salt.
Piper loved the sand
Between her toes.
Piper was a music maker.
Piper loved chocolate.
Piper was a person who played the bagpipes.
Piper was Einstein.
Piper was the Cookie Monster.
Piper was Saturn.
Piper was Ms. Rodriguez and
Piper was the alphabet.
Piper was the dwarf planet but Lily,
Lily would be a groovy girl.
Lily, a taller reflection.
Lily, an idol.
Lily wouldn't hobble. Lily would float
Gracefully on the fresh water.
Lily, with the still water.
Lily would be soft, green moss.
Piper was a pink flamingo who hopped and hobbled but
Lily, she would never sink.
Lily, she would never pop.
Lily would be so agreeable.
Before heading out to some drive-in movie or something
With some mop-haired someone or other,
Lily would breathe
Rosemary scented air
Into hydrated petals,
Hydrated lungs.
Lily would be the language of love.

Lily would be the love of language.
Lily would be so agréable.
La, le, les.
L'amour.
Samuels has been around the world.
More than once.
Samuels was a man.
Samuels is stern and a bit intimidating.
Samuels will be confident.
Samuels is loud and
Quiet, too.
Samuels will wear a tie and a brown tweed blazer,
Samuels, the kind with patches on the elbows
Fit for arm-wrestling.
A handshake battle.
Samuels is king of the handshake.
Get over here, Samuels!
Samuels bought a timeshare.
Samuels has been to Paris.
Samuels has been to Paris on a business trip and
Samuels goes because he enjoys the coffee.
Le café.
Samuels is old.
Samuels had memory.
Samuels is memory.
Samuels brings his daughters to a steakhouse,
Orders them salads.
Samuels brings his daughters to a steakhouse,
Filet and a scotch for Samuels, thanks.
And when the meal is over
And when it's cold and drizzly outside,
Samuels will throw on a black nylon raincoat
Overtop his brown tweed blazer
And button up, hiding
Three little penguins
Stacked and hungry,
Yearning to unbutton
And topple over
Onto freshly paved sand.
A good name would.

An Open Letter to Eowyn of Rohan, Regarding the Amazingness of Her Hair

Rivka Crowbourne

Dear Mrs. Faramir:

Congratulations on your recent nuptials! It was a lovely wedding—obviously less lovely than Arwen and Aragorn's, but lovelier than Samwise and Rosie's by several tactfully understated orders of magnitude. And although one might quibble over the precise definition of "something borrowed," it's nice that you found a way of upcycling the Witch-King's kneecaps.

And, speaking of everyone's favorite ex-Nazgul—can we talk about your hair? Seconds before you-*go*-girling your opponent in his event horizon of a face, you doffed your helmet to reveal quite possibly the most luminous tresses this side of Numenor. I venture to touch on the subject because, despite my resorting to such extreme measures as occasionally *not* riding a horse for three full days with a steel pot on my head and then fighting elephants for an hour and a half, my own hair seems borderline frumpy next to yours.

Am I going about the whole thing wrong? Should I forgo shampoo and curlers in favor of tactical anti-pachyderm close-quarters combat? Is there some secret virtue in smelted haberdashery that brings out the luster in one's locks? Perhaps the intense heat and pressure of trapped sweat fuses the sedimentary layers of hair into an obscure species of diamond, radiating feminine perfection when exposed to wraiths on smelly pterodactyls. Perhaps—just as the color we see in a physical object is actually the one color reflected *away* from that object—if one's scalp becomes sufficiently unkempt, beauty bounces off it and becomes the attractive blonde photons that strike the retinas of outside observers. This hypothesis gains credence from the fact that your brother Eomer, who (presumably) spends even less time on his coiffure than you, has amazing hair as well. It could be sheer genetics, I suppose, but even Gimli turns out to be primed for GQ on the rare occasions when he de-helmets.

Is it the pipe-weed? It's the pipe-weed, isn't it! Theoden, of course, was unac-
quainted with hobbitic smoking habits—but *you* had Meriadoc in your saddle
the whole way to Minas Tirith, hot-boxing you with second-hand fumes.
Could Longbottom Leaf be the key to healthy follicles? The anti-tobacco lobby is not going to like this, Mrs. Faramir. Nor will my pulmonary apparatus
thank you for my new practice of vaping into a hardhat on the way to work.

But I really mustn't put the blame on you. Clearly, you just can't help having
infinitely gorgeous hair at all times, no matter how hard you try. It must be a
terrible burden. Well, I've taken enough of your time. I hope your husband
enjoys *not being King of Gondor.*

Yours very truly,

R.C.

Flan

Alla Vilnyanskaya

After Frank O'Hara

Let's say you like flan
And the last time you ate flan
You ended up in the hospital
Then you see flan again
And you still like flan
But you don't want to be in the hospital
You can't eat flan again
And not get sick

Ford Focus

Alla Vilnyanskaya

I.
This poem is called
take me
instead
Take me instead
though I am no longer (whatever classic thing they say
about aging)

The burden of action
rests unfortunately on the heads of those who know

II.
I no longer give out my poems for free
am no longer circling Villanova campus
In my Ford Focus

My father, who told me, well
I guess in the end he didn't really say much

Your Turn to Deal

Eric Diamond

At our stage of Life,
      we gather
      to speak the unspoken.

We know
      what Time does,

the life force, at play,

      to amuse, or distract,

to defy emptiness,

      to be teased by permanence—

The numbers
on the obituary pages
say it plain:

      71, 83, 66 *(mighty uncomfortable)*,
      77, 94 *(reassuring)*, 47 *(why?)*,
      99 *(ah, yes)*, 68….

(and yet),
one continues
      to create.

A text comes through:
We have a seat at the table—
      bring some cards—
            we want to take your money—

Like the old folks
      used to say:

"It's good to be alive"

An Act of Kindness

Murzban F. Shroff

She was not planning to go home today, her husband would be there, he'd be drinking, he'd get drunk, after some time his friends would arrive, he'd be pleased to see them, he'd offer them a drink, they'd accept, as though they could refuse, after some time they'd get drunk, they'd call to her, she should come and join them, but seeing her silence they'd ask if there was anything to eat, anything fresh and tasty from her hands, and in asking they'd be polite, they would be sincere, till she came and served them, then they'd get touchy, friendly, as though she was their property, their *maal*, and her husband would be watching, his eyes fixed on her sad frozen face, reading her thoughts and wondering if she knew what was expected, if she would respond, somewhat.

He was not an unpleasant man, nor was he a bully. He spoke very little, and that made her feel she did not know him. Besides, he was older, shorter, and thick at the waist.

He was an important man: that much she knew. He worked at the municipality, and people came to see him. They came with their problems and sometimes their tears. And he heard them and assured them their problems would be solved. But first, some money had to change hands. Money and favors. The money he locked away in a safe behind the temple. The favors would have to be delivered over time, he said. He smiled when he said that, a slow unctuous smile. His friends, the regulars, they came home to see him, and sometimes her, she suspected.

She was attractive, mature at thirty. Age refused to show on her. She would never be a mother, she knew, but that did not bother her. She wondered, though, if he ever thought of it, if he ever regretted their marriage. But they had never spoken of it, never spoken of anything except her duties around the house. That was spelled out the day she got married.

She did not mind the housework, did not mind the silence of the large, empty house. The housework kept her feeling young, energetic, and useful, and the silence left her free to dream.

What did she dream about? What kind of daydreams, precisely? Nothing much, nothing out of the ordinary. She wished she could be like the women in the TV serials she watched. She wished she could dress like them, talk like them; she had the love and admiration of a large family who lived together in a large house, who celebrated birthdays and festivals.

She knew she could manage such a family. She could plan to a budget, run a tight kitchen, put three hearty meals on the table, please all the family members all the time. She had the strength and the build for that.

In her father's house, there had been just her, her father, and her brother, who sat slumped in a chair, staring into space and dribbling saliva onto his chest. She remembered getting a napkin and placing it across his chest, so that his shirt would not get stained. But when she would raise the napkin to his lips, her brother would turn his head and scream so loudly that her father would come running and accuse her of trying to harm him. Then she would step back, confused, while her brother would shiver and slowly wet his pants. She realized, at some point, that it was the roughness of the napkin that bothered him. His facial skin was like tissue: daubed, it would turn pink; rubbed, it would start peeling. She did not know what he was like inside, but she could guess: a tangle of nerves, all frayed and twisted. He was older than her by four years but had always been like this, and nothing could help him.

How could she have a child after this? How could she even dream of it? Thank God her husband had that problem. She could always say it was God's will; it was not meant to be.

She knew what her father had been through with her brother. Why he held onto his job as a manual scavenger, lowering himself daily, into drains and gutters, into the gases and smells of the city. Why he drank every evening till he passed out. Or why he stood in the doorway, looking at his son and crying softly, sometimes raising his hands and apologizing.

Her mother had died because she couldn't cope with the situation. Because she knew when failure was staring her in the face. The failure to produce a normal child, a son with emotions, feelings, dreams, hopes any parent would have.

Her youth had been spent looking after her brother. On cooking for him, feeding him, bathing him, helping him with his toilet duties, cleaning up after him. Later, carrying him to bed when he wanted to sleep.

It was just as well that she was built like a man and had the strength of one. That would make men stare at her. First with disbelief, then with lust. She knew they were imagining themselves with her. She knew what was going through their heads, the scoundrels! The devils!

Sometimes she felt guilty looking at her brother. What should have gone to him, rightfully, had come to her: the looks, the strength, the height, the ability to feel pain by virtue of being normal. In his case, *nothing*. Nothing would register, nothing would be felt or expressed. He had no sense of right or wrong, no concept of good or evil.

Sometimes she'd be tempted to topple him from his chair. To throw him facedown and see if he'd respond. She wanted to see him struggle to his feet. She wanted to see him try and stand. She wanted to see—just effort. But to him, sitting and standing and waking and sleeping were one and the same. It was as though his birth were a sentence for others—a life sentence in a maximum-security prison.

But now she knew what had to be done. A plan was in place, and it was unfolding behind those doors. Those great white doors, with men in green robes and green masks, who always seemed to be in a hurry and had little to say.

She wondered what kind of a man he'd have been, had he been normal.

Would he have been funny and intelligent? Or would he have been sober?

Would he have taken up for her against her father when he said all those harsh things to her? When he abused her, cursed her, and called her a jinx? At six feet four inches, she made men look feeble; she made them appear small in their own eyes. That's how it was even when she had won the hurdles in school: she had been asked not to take her place on the victory stand; she was not allowed to trumpet her win in public.

But: Would her brother have chosen a groom for her personally, checking out the family and their background?

Would he have married her into a good family, where people would have understood her?

Would he have been a pillar to her, a foil to her husband and his friends?

Would he have protected her as Lord Laxmana had protected Lord Rama?

But why brood over things that weren't meant to be? Why accuse her father of what was her destiny? He'd had a hard time, too, managing without a wife, then borrowing large sums of money to keep his son alive.

Besides, it hadn't been easy to find a groom for her. The men she liked didn't like looking up to her. And after a while, her opinion didn't seem to matter. She knew what the verdict was even before it was delivered. *Thoda jyada tall hain*, the boy's parents would say. As though they were anguished by the decision they'd made. As though they were giving up on her, reluctantly.

Sometimes she felt the body she carried wasn't hers. It was a body that drew excitement, curiosity, lust, pity. The lust she saw in every man's eyes.

Every man except her husband. And the pity she saw in other women's eyes. The same kind of pity when they looked at her brother.

And now, her husband was plotting against her. To give away her body without her consent. To quench other men's thirst because he couldn't drink at her pool. From father to husband, she could see the type of man she had drawn. One who couldn't keep her for himself, so he passed her on to others. There was no use crying about this, no use brooding. It was just the way things had turned out for her.

***

Raani from Andheri was not a woman you or I could have known. We might have passed her on the streets and glanced at her with surprise. We might have seen her on a bus or a train and marveled at her height. We might have run into her in the bazaar, where the vendors would eye her slyly. We might have spotted her at a beauty pageant, sashaying onto the stage, thrusting her hips at the audience, then turning and walking away, a smile playing at the corners of her mouth. But because we didn't know her personally, we can never quite understand what she did.

How on earth could she turn her brother over to a clinic?

How on earth could she agree to a price on both his kidneys?

How could she tell her father that they would be taking just one kidney and that the money from that would clear all his debts?

How could she convince her father that older patients had survived on one kidney for the rest of their lives? And that one less kidney meant less bed wettings and less work.

Raani from Andheri was not a woman you or I could have known. We might have seen her in a bar and considered her shrewdly. Or spotted her at the gym, smiling and chewing up the treadmill. Or sat next to her on a flight and allowed ourselves a little conversation, a mild flirtation. But we could never have understood why she did what she did.

How could she take her father's signature on a form, making him responsible if the surgery failed?

How could she take all that money, knowing it came at the price of her conscience?

How could she wheel her brother down that corridor with the smell of antiseptic in her nose?

How could she remove the napkin from his chest in a way he wouldn't notice?

How could she stop outside the operating theater and kiss him lightly on the forehead, knowing it was the last touch of kindness he'd feel?

All Love Poems Are Horror Poems When You Are The Creature: A Contrapuntal in 3 Parts

R. Thursday

monsters -	like me -	I deserve
love, i'm told,	as much as	anyone willing -
different	names mostly fit -	but scared -
- is it always so	so wrong to want	to be
someone's	creature -	called
not alone?	creation	of course -
requires	i walk	liminal and
light	through	unpainted
shattering;	my lover's	hands
gentle -	eyes:	suture-soft
and i	hold no	stitches
unoffered:	mirrors	and metaphors;
still	to define	new borders - i mean
breaths -	myself inside	the disordered parts -
how	like a vampire -	unbeaten but
afraid	here	i might resurrect through
your lightning,	i want	a switch -
Would bring	your heart	closer to
me awake.	more.	alive

Listen to Gala's Mutterings

Sylvia Anne Telfer

Earth in crisis. Solution essential. Scan heavens
for *deus ex machina*. Nil. Pleading letter vital
but where's messenger, stamp, address for appeal?
Wormhole sky and Crow about. Eureka!
Crow's Keeper of the Sacred Law. Send Crow!
Sky's alchemical, a path to infinity and Crow,
at our beg, now in postie haul.
Crow, can you truly wing back that essential reply?
Too lean sack to be worthy?
No two-way traffic, even 'return to sender' flack?
Crow, you angle to where 21st century sky vanishes
in a sort of crow 'Bermuda Triangle' bending laws
of physical universe, and I recall with fear Ted Hughes
wrote in creative burn that crow flew only
the black flag of himself.
So, Crow, you mightn't be in our narrative of return,
even shrugged off postie gear, and why have old
polestar values fled and must we thus metamorphose
into Super Heroes minus cape, unable to fly after them?
Besides, will we be able to distinguish between
dialogue and monologue? If not, maybe no voices
and we're merely ventriloquists reading out ancient
diaries written by strangers—maybe now even third-person.
Do we really think we can find answers 'up there'
or un-sky a god who'll solve all?
Where's Crow? Forgotten mission? Maybe for he's no
sense of time, sees past, present and future in chorus.
In Crow awaital, today's icons fail as default mode
and thus possible [alike Crow no-show] sanity's
poof- gone in prejudices clomping in worn-out shoes,
in latest twitter inanity, grooming of Facebook profile,
'essential shopping' translating to bags of designer gear.

Illusion's parochial, inside linear time and outside
'Go with flow for tomorrow's never promised!'
Crow may never return for postage underpaid
and so we must ourselves unearth black box
of original human psyche from which we've strayed.

Below, the aftermath:
Yet smells wet rock in shaft, burning flesh when candles
ignited in "firedamp", recalls cave-in terror.
He now questions why he was underground, a miner.
Coal dust, trillions of crows in rookery of lungs,
Blessing or curse trees pressed into coal seams
that in "The Valleys" of Wales of mammoth depth?
Many "Valley Boys" bulldozed into pits—kinship with trees
in that 'no choice', and such emptying of soul in valleys
echoing thump of engines, cranks of coal-heavy cages.
Had ancient trees mourned themselves?
Had any miner mourned a lost self?
Why had there never been other identities?
Green female face sprouting greenery's peering from shrub.
Trick of light? Gypsy woman?
Only heard of a Green Man through airy-fairy mam
babbling it was ancient guardian of forest whose
green skin smothered in oak leaf, acorn.
Tetchy over scorn, she'd scolded it was the wilderness,
the primeval, the keeper of holiness of forest.
Still, such a rough dance when Green Man's
foliate head in stone churches deemed dated, and erased.
So, Green Man lost his home.
How many miners in pit closures lost theirs?
More kinship.
Pluck of harp. Odd it sounds like The Taff
—resonant, drifting, then rushing, splashing, cascading.
                    God's many voices? Or is it wind?
Suddenly, Green Woman's gone.
Is she 'The Lady of the North' carved into hill, and who must
now be walking miles of paths winding around knolls,
marshes, between ridges to once again be colossal languishing
female formed from clay, dirt, slag-waste from Shotton Mine?

Is she conscience of mine owner, a prayer
to offset harm done in stripping land for coal?
Is he himself violator or, in this epiphany, convert?
A return to his Catholic Church,
(Yr Eglwys Gatholig yng Nghymru a Lloegr)?
Even gone back to his roots for foliage is issuing
from his mouth as if he's fusing with soil?
Now and then, something holy allows a fresh budding.

        PURE   CANE
        ONLY   FELL
        FROMrefineROWSsugars
        IN Ato buyLANDwar ONcunningham EXPANDING THE MILL,
OF   HEATin theTHENday OFgrowth IFpowdering the swamp,
THE CANE FILLED OYSTER CREEKuntil the rise of an
WITH BROKEN STALK AND BROKENobnoxious creek sold
BACK A SWEET TIME WOULD COMEthe town up river to
TO FILL THE LAND WITH BROKENan alligator, who on
HOMES.   KEMPNER, THE RAMBLERa muddy street asked
USHERING IN SWEET TIMES, SATon the status of the
UPON THE CREEK TO SINK BRICKsweet meats sloshing
NEXT TO GLASS, STEEL WELDINGthrough and dropping
THE FLOW OF KEEP AND BURDEN.in the liquid paths.
TERRY'S SWAMP SWEETENED WITHthen the sweet crack
SWEAT SALTING THE MULE STONEof the bat as a ball
FOR THE TURN OF THE CRUSHINGsailed, crossing the
STALK.   CATHOLIC, METHODIST,office of nolan ryan
PRESBYTERIAN, ECUMENISM FULLand the boys hailing
OF MAHOGONY AND THE IMPERIALfrom alvin, hoarding
INN'S ORNATE FIRE.   FOOTBALLthe air space as all
FUMBLED ITS WAY INTO THEATREthe oxygen was stole
AND FIELD, SHOPPING FOR THATfrom near the lacing
CENTER FLOWERING SUGAR LAND.on its flight south.

The Poorfolk of Poorbury
B. Elliott Crist

The Messenger

Catherine Shields

My cousin Charlie and I stand six feet apart in my living room. I imagine he has already calculated the prescribed distance before he even stepped over the threshold. He hasn't changed. Not since I saw him ten years ago when he came to my wedding and wore what seemed to be an exact replica of that long, black coat.

When he called to say he was coming to Florida and asked if he could visit, I agreed. Of course, I agreed: He's my cousin; he's family. But now that he's here, I realize it was a mistake. I should have made up an excuse or told him we'd be out of town.

Now Charlie strokes his long beard and sways from side to side. The tzitzit, knotted ritual strings, peek beneath his jacket hem and dance along with him. I imagine rivulets of sweat pooling beneath the layers of his heavy clothing and wonder if he'll take off the coat. I bet he'll keep it on. It stays.

Years ago, we were friends. I've never told him otherwise. He wouldn't understand. But his visit reminds me of how close we were when we were growing up, roaming the Miami neighborhood like wild monkeys, pulling mangoes off the trees and launching imaginary grenades. Charlie, wild and willing to take all kinds of risks, charmed everyone. People turned toward him like sunflowers following the light, whereas I was introverted, shy, and awkward. Friends were hard to come by but Charlie dragged me along to parties where I'd do my best wallflower routine. I loved watching the faces of entranced listeners whenever he shared one of my stories. At one of those parties, Charlie introduced me to my future husband, Andrew.

After I met Andrew, the three of us rented a house and became adventuresome explorers who did everything together. Bike rides, rock concerts, traveling to rallies to protest the War, we had our sights set on finishing our last year of school so we could go out into the world and practice the art of adulting. We called ourselves The Three Musketeers. When we graduated from college, we took a road trip across the country, one last hurrah before settling into planned careers.

One night, as we sat by the fire, Charlie talked about his desperate search for life's meaning. He was serious about joining the Hare Krishnas, who had danced through our college campus. I made fun of him, not realizing

Charlie teetered on the edge of his decision to leave everything behind and join them.

"You'd never do that. You're a Jewish boy," I scoffed. But Andrew believed he was serious. An hour earlier, we had taken the LSD Charlie had offered. The campfire crackled as we tripped, and I leaned back to view the sky, not paying any attention to the boys as they traveled down mystical rabbit holes, discussing philosophy and the meaning of life.

I remember Andrew said, "If you want spirituality, why not seek it in Jewish mysticism?" Years later, I would blame him for pointing my cousin in that direction.

Near the end of that summer, in 1984, Charlie disappeared. For the next six months, we didn't hear from him. I wrote long, rambling letters that went unanswered. I wondered if he *had* run off and joined a cult. His mother, my Aunt Helen, informed me Charlie had enrolled in a yeshiva, to study ancient Judaism. When Andrew proposed, I tasked Aunt Helen with the delivery of his wedding invitation, elated when she told me he would attend along with the rest of the family.

"But I have to warn you," she added, "Charlie has become *observant.*" What did that mean? The way she whispered the word 'observant' sounded foreboding.

Two days before the ceremony, Andrew and I headed to the hotel where everyone had booked rooms. When the door opened, I rushed toward my cousin. "Charlie!" I cried.

He took a step back and held one hand up as if to say, *don't come any closer.* He looked so different. Gone were the flannel shirts, baseball caps, and jeans, replaced with a long, jet-black coat and black fedora. He had cut his long hair short except for the *payos,* which curled in tendrils down his neck. White fringe hung from the top of his pants and trailed halfway down. My cousin looked as if he had stepped out of the eighteenth century.

"Please call me Chaim. That's my Hebrew name." His hand hovered in the air, warding off my impending embrace. "I am not permitted to touch women."

I dropped my hands to my side. The ground between us split. A gaping crevasse. Charlie–Chaim–whoever this was, hooked both thumbs into the pockets of his long black coat. Then he grabbed Andrew. They thumped each other on the back while I stood alone, a pariah.

***

Now, ten years later, my cousin, the stranger, stands beside me in my living room. I try not to think about that moment when everything changed, or how I've missed him, or how I feel that rumble of hope every year when we get mail from Crown Heights, even though I know it will just be a packet of prayers for an upcoming Jewish holiday. Warily, I gesture at the sofa and suggest we sit. Chaim chooses the tan lounge chair, settles in, and drapes a hand over the edge of the armrest. Trying to be an accommodating hostess, I offer him snacks I'd set out, but he declines. Shame brightens my cheeks as I stare at my bag of chips poured into my non-kosher bowl, rendering it inedible. I had forgotten about his dietary restrictions. Andrew jumps into action, offering to go on a kosher grocery run.

Paper goods too, Chaim requests. He can't eat from our dishes. I can't justify my anger, but it flares up before I can stifle it. Andrew takes off, and I regret I didn't volunteer. I'm uncertain how to entertain my cousin or what topics are off-limits. But as we sit across from each other, my four-year-old daughter, Tessa, stares at the stranger with her brown, almond-shaped eyes. Born with Down syndrome, sometimes she has trouble keeping her pink glasses on her face. Before she stands, she pushes them over the flat bridge of her nose. She's headed for Chaim, her eyes locked on the fringe, but I intercept her before she can reach him. I glance up and mumble, "Sorry about that."

My cousin's laughing blue eyes flash beneath the brim of his hat. Apparently, Tessa has amused him. I spot my cousin's crooked smile peeking through the bushy beard. Charlie always had a smile that seemed to hold a secret, one he couldn't wait to spill.

Chaim lifts a hand and strokes his beard while he watches me redirect Tessa. "I see why my mother admires you. But I'd like to ask, do you know the word *neshama*? It's Hebrew. It means soul."

I shrug and shift uncomfortably in my seat. A tiny part of me had hoped that this visit would differ from the yearly prayer packets, but that spark quickly dims.

"Neshama," I repeat. "Why do you ask?"

He nods excitedly and tells me about the Rebbe as he leans forward, hands clasped in front of him like he's ready to deliver an important message.

"The Rebbe is renowned for his gift as a storyteller. He always has the right message to deliver to those who suffer."

"Why, who do you think is suffering?"

Chaim's eyes remain on Tessa. "Many parents come to the Rebbe for advice when they have a child with special needs. He would say Tessa is a treasured gift given because you and Andrew were deemed worthy."

"Thanks." I offer, although I'm not grateful. I'm sick of hearing these blanket statements about children with disabilities. He probably intended this

as a compliment, it comes across as a meaningless platitude. My cousin bobs
his head like one of those dolls in the tourist shops.

"You're welcome." He tells me Tessa is a highly evolved soul who has
chosen to become human. An angel incarnate. "Children like Tessa are born
with souls that possess a tremendous amount of light, with a magnitude that's
so great it causes the vessel to crack and break."

What do you mean 'the vessel,' her body?"

Chaim nods. "The Rebbe would say her *neshama* is a brilliant light that
shines through the cracks."

"Cracks? She isn't broken."

He prattles on. "Tessa has a childlike spirit. What more could a mother
wish for than her child to be happy? You have been blessed." He flashes his
crooked grin, which only raises my hackles.

"Tessa is no more or less a blessing than any other child." I try to keep
the annoyance out of my voice and don't bother explaining that I've heard
similar stories from mothers of children with Down syndrome and that many
of them have called our kids blessings. There's no point arguing that *all*
children are a blessing or that both mothers *and* fathers want their children to
be happy. Chaim might not care what I think. He was always a better speaker
than listener. But now there is a wall between us that cannot be breached, and
I am very much alone. I shouldn't have expected this visit to be different from
the last time I saw my cousin in this garb.

Andrew calls from the kitchen, announcing he's back. He walks into the
living room, carrying a tray of the approved snacks. Before he plops down
beside Chaim, they embrace. That's when my eyes fill with tears. It hurts to
watch the two of them. I get up from my seat and scoop up Tessa.

"It's bedtime. Be right back."

Andrew lifts an eyebrow and gives me a knowing look.

Instead of going to bed, I carry Tessa outside. Her petite body curves
into mine as I stare at the night sky, remembering another night sky bedecked
with stars. It occurs to me that there may be some mystical force at play.

Perhaps Chaim believes God sent him to deliver a message, but he didn't
need to tell me Tessa is special. I already know that. The actual message is
Charlie has found what he was looking for.

I should be happy for him.

Even if I'm not.

Sci(na)ku Poetry

Roxanne Barbour

well-being
offworlder topic
differing from humans

news of infection
affecting humans
tri-color
skin blossoming
often denoting flags

stages of illness
infecting Martians
cancer
different forms
humans assisting research

Precipice

Jeffrey Dieter

The mind standing at the edge
of itself looks back at windows and waits,
disregards the green water blown back and forth,
the weed tangled otters.
What the windows say she cannot hear,
hearing instead a primacy of dislocation,
a hall full of mirrors and faces she will not meet.

The mind standing at the edge
of itself sees the body as meat, dressed or undressed,
sits beside herself as no self would see.
What could she be today besides a thing, waiting,
a stone marked by stones?

Once she sang at the top of herself—
giving over her body to body
just to hear a child sing.
He came yellow, blowing cataract-blue,
blooming on white sheets.

I Was Told "Never Again"

Abigail Boyer

The news plays the headlining story: another school shooting. This time Uvalde, Texas. Pictures of children who are now dead. Interviews with parents struggling with life. Clips of fifth-graders recounting how they survived. Voices of parents explaining how part of them died too. Tears well in my eyes, my cheeks turning pink with heat. I go for a walk.

I deviate from my normal walking path along the bay. I weave my way through the neighborhood I've grown up in, turning right at the park, then left at my childhood best friend's house, continuing straight past the crazy cat lady's house. I know full well where I am going but am denying it to myself. I am supposed to be walking to clear my mind, not to further the pain.

I don't expect to cry so much when I see it – my elementary school. But the closer I get, the quicker the tears fall. I find myself thinking back to my innocence at the time. Within those walls I dreamed infinitely. I dreamed about who I was going to become without considering expectations. I dreamed about being a tour guide without weighing the salary. I dreamed of having ten dogs not knowing it's illegal. I dreamed about falling in love without thinking about heartbreak. I dreamed of growing up without worrying about getting old. I dreamed about flying without the fear of falling.

Within those walls I also did my first active shooter drill. I was taught to run under the red dot on the ceiling, get down, sit still, be silent, don't cry because that makes noise, make sure the teacher calls 911, close the windows, shut the blinds, lock the door, turn off the lights, and wait for the police. The importance of every step was ingrained into me, it was life or death. Unlike fires and earthquakes, shooters did discriminate. Don't be the easy target. I was nine at the time. Sandy Hook taught us we had to be prepared.

I continue to walk around the school, avoiding any eye contact with strangers. I don't want to have to explain my tears. I shouldn't worry adults and can't worry kids. I pull the sleeve of my sweatshirt over my hand to wipe the tears, but try to disguise it as rubbing dust out of my eye. I look at the posters in the classroom windows. Crayon drawings that had yet to face the criticism of the real world. These classrooms are a bubble in today's world, a rare space where it is okay to fail and the attempt is always praised. I pass the mural of otters, the school's mascot, made by kids a few years older than me. The mural was their graduating project, a thank you gift to their community.

The colors are now quite faded. My class made a mural too, but you can't see it from the outside of the school. By the posters hanging on the gates I see that this year's graduating class has taken a different approach to their community thank you gift. They're raising two-thousand twenty-two dollars for the local food bank as the class of two-thousand twenty-two. I pull out my phone, scan the QR code, and donate. I recognize that I'm doing this to make myself feel better. Like maybe through a donation I can help return innocence to these children. I know that isn't how it works, but I donate anyway.

My elementary school doesn't entirely look the same as when I left though. While the buildings are still a faded yellow and the wall-ball courts are still a forest green, the short chain-link fence that was meant to keep kids in has now been replaced by a tall black steel-barred fence with locking gates that are meant to keep others out. I stop on a patch of grass between the sidewalk and the fence. I look in at the school. Tears still fall from my eyes. It was here, after Sandy Hook, when I was told, "never again." Adults trying to ease my mind, and theirs. The red dot on the ceiling was "just in case." But nearly ten years later, the threat hasn't ceased, we've just tried to adapt.

I've spent over seven years in school since Sandy Hook, and continue to in college. I've mastered the art of running and hiding under the red dot, sitting in a fearful silence, quickly turning off lights, dodging out of view from the window, and being prepared to push desks against the door in case I'm the next target. When my mind wanders in class, it's no longer to my dreams, it's to what I would do. Do I hide or run? Where would be the best place to hide? Can a bullet go through a metal desk? What can easily be pushed against the door? Do I know how to open the window? Will I break a leg jumping out a two-story window? Can you run on a broken leg? Do I help others or put myself first? What's the quickest way out of the building? Is it better to run straight or zig zag? Is it worth trying to grab my phone? How will my parents know I love them?

I find myself still crying, but no longer at the loss of my innocence. I am crying for the loss of innocence of these young children. Their wide-eyed wonder for the world has been shattered from bullets. Their rose-colored glasses are no longer rosy, rather red from the blood of their peers. My mind flashes back to the news. The images of smiling children who were murdered. The reality is even the children who survive will still have scars. If not physical, mental. I'm clearly struggling to process this, and I'm nineteen years old and thousands of miles away from where the bullets rained. I can't imagine seeing bodies on the ground, hearing the stream of bullets, or facing the loss of empty classrooms and lost friends.

Solitary Musings

Maroula Blades

For once, at least, the sun rises to shine; it's spring.
Official orders, "Self-isolate or risk contagion."
My ritual *latte* has to wait or be cut for good.
The walks I promised myself are parading thoughts.

Official orders, "Self-isolate or risk contagion."
I shuffle from the unmade bed to the kitchen and back.
The walks I promised myself are parading thoughts.
Is this the flu I'm feeling? On CNN, I saw the count.

I shuffle from the unmade bed to the kitchen and back.
Heat kills COVID-19. I hunch over a bowl of steaming water.
Is this the flu I'm feeling? On CNN, I saw the count.
My head slumps like a clump of tabloid papier mâché.

Heat kills COVID-19. I hunch over a bowl of steaming water.
The mind is foggier than the rising menthol mist.
My head slumps like a clump of tabloid papier mâché.
Ten hours to pass before bedtime, solitary confinement.

My mind is foggier than the rising menthol mist.
I need groceries. Should a friend make a visit?
Ten hours to pass before bedtime, solitary confinement.
The clock's second hand turns in slow motion.

I need groceries. Should a friend make a visit?
Mum's voice echoes, "Don't feed the bug."
The clock's second hand turns in slow motion.
A film shows how to paint, like Franz Kline. I love his *Chief,* 1950.

Mum's voice echoes, "Don't feed the bug."
On a cross-like easel sits a virgin cotton canvas.
A film shows how to paint, like Franz Kline. I love his *Chief,* 1950.
From a *Lamp Black* lid, paint dribbles.

On a cross-like easel sits a virgin cotton canvas.
My ritual *latte* has to wait or be cut for good.
From a *Lamp Black* lid, paint dribbles.
For once, at least, the sun rises to shine; it's spring.

Family Feed
Silke Heiss

Young girl buck –
you draw my love!

Standing on your knock-kneed stilts,
white-painted shins –
mastering the avocado peels,
leaves of leek and cores of pears –

positioning all, with deft thrusts
of neck and chin, so your teeth,
at the back of your long mouth,
can at last get a grip.

You stare, chewing, dreamy-eyed, at me
– what a breakfast,
on dewy grass in winter sun!

Fetching for me the infinite,
ungulate patience of your kind,
so I may apply it
to our greater family,
and feed them too.

Waiting

Miki Lentin

Fatima stood perfectly still by the front door, breathing, but not noticeably, as if the stuffing had been sucked out of her. She squeezed her arms into her chest. Her headscarf, wrapped tight in layers and folds around her head and neck, dripped from the rain.

"You're wet, do you want a towel?" I asked from the bottom of the stairs.

She didn't blink, like she was fixating her gaze on something through me.

"It's late, have you been at the mosque?" I asked. It was unusual for her to come home after eleven thirty.

Her forehead was creased with concern.

"Did the bus go on one of those detours again?" I laughed, "I told you the trains are quicker. Remember?"

Rain drummed onto the roof. A siren faded in the distance.

"Do you want to sit down?" I suggested.

She flashed a glance in my direction and remained standing. A circle of water formed around her on the doormat. I yawned, and motioned as if I was about to go upstairs.

"Cat," she said. It sounded like ket, the k and t punctuating the silence, as if she was spitting out the word. "Black cat. Outside," she said. Her accent Eritrean Arabic.

"Oh, that one. Yeh, bloody thing's always there."

"One hour I wait, outside," she said. "One hour. Ooofff." She exhaled sharply, her chest deflating.

Fat, bulging and black, like a rain cloud, there's a stray cat that likes to hold court on the wall by the gate to our house. Because I'm allergic I usually give it a wide berth or flick my foot at it. It scampers, but always returns, and waits outside our house, as if it *wants* to mess with me.

"Would you like some tea?" I asked. Fatima liked a glass of black tea late at night. She'd wait for the sugar cubes to completely dissolve before sipping it. She said it helped her sleep.

"Why the black cat no move? I move." She jabbed herself in the chest.

"I move to the other side of the road. I cross the road. I stand by the next house. I stand by the car. Ooofff." Her arms fell by her side. "I walk to the shop. I come back. Cat still there." She pursed her lips.

"I'm not sure I understand. I squinted my itchy eyes, trying to concentrate. Are you scared of cats?"

"No," she exclaimed, and leant back, affronted by the question.

"Bloody thing. Why didn't you just shoo it away?"

"Shoo?" she looked at me quizzically.

I flicked my hand. "You know, shoo."

"No shoo. This cat not moving." She wagged her finger exactingly.

"But, why didn't you text or call me? I would have shoo-ed it away and let you in."

She didn't respond. We stood in silence for a few moments, the only sound the dishwasher beeping, once, twice, three times.

I couldn't drop it.

"But…" I mumbled impatiently. I wanted a proper answer. I knew Fatima didn't mind waiting, but for an hour?

She often told me how long it took her to travel to her appointments by bus. Two and a half hours on the 91, 59 and 109 to the Home Office in Croydon, two hours on the W7, 253 and 308 to the Refugee Council in Stratford and seventy-five minutes on the 41 and 231 to English ESOL level two at Enfield College. I imagined her waiting to change buses, sitting awkwardly on the narrow plastic benches, checking Citymapper every few minutes, wrapping her hoodie around her thin body, calculating the travel time.

"They're so unreliable," I huffed one evening after she'd told me that she'd waited forty-five minutes for a 91.

"But you can see, outside," she said, her voice rising. "Underground," she wagged her finger, "No good, like a cave."

"Is there a reason you don't like black cats?"

"Reason?" she asked.

"Yeh, like in your culture?"

I grabbed my phone and typed, "Eritrean cat superstition." Nothing much came up. I banged the screen again, "black cat pavement Eritrea." A few pages appeared with images of pavements and pedestrian crossings in Eritrea. One last go. "Black cat Eritrean culture." Little apart from some videos and cutesy photos of black kittens. I smiled apologetically, and stuffed my phone into my pocket.

"Did you have a bad experience with a cat?"

"Me? No," she said, "I like cats. This cat sit outside the house. This cat looking at me. This cat not let me pass. This cat not happy, she shook her head. No, no, no." That wagging finger again. "Me," she put her hands on her chest, "I like cats. Not this cat. So…" she paused, "I wait."

Don't, I said to myself, as I itched to ask again what she did outside for an hour, in the rain, when she could have shoo-ed the cat away, and been in bed by now, drinking her tea, planning tomorrow's bus journeys. Don't, I thought, tell her that you are allergic to cats and have the test results to prove it. Don't tell her that your tear ducts swell when you go near them. Don't tell her that you used to throw water at cats in the garden, and scream obscenities at them. Don't tell her that you enjoy hissing at that black cat that sits outside the house.

She slipped off her trainers and walked towards the kitchen, her feet leaving wet footprints on the floor.

The kettle roared.

I needed an explanation, but why now? I wasn't an asylum seeker like Fatima. I hadn't lived on the streets for eight years since I was eighteen. I hadn't left my family behind in Eritrea. I hadn't begged for food and water. I hadn't had to wait for answers from the Home Office. I hadn't lost contact with everyone I knew because I'd lost all my phone numbers. I had never been reliant on charity. I didn't have to wait in line, often for hours when I needed new clothes. I hadn't spent an hour outside a house that was hosting an asylum seeker trying to get in, but found the entrance blocked, by a black cat.

I removed a couple of mugs from the cupboard, made two teas, and pulled out a chair for Fatima at the table.

We sat down. She dropped a couple of sugar cubes into her cup. I waited.

Please Stop Calling This Spontaneous Abortion

Jill Michelle

What the doctors call
spontaneous abortion—
forty mornings of
linens stained red, your child dead
no matter your intentions.

The Faultline

Frederick Pollack

I knew he was dead, but apparently
there had been a misunderstanding
or special dispensation or general
amnesty; you'd think that would be
what we talked about, but the issue
was lost in my joy at seeing him again
and picking up where we'd left off
(which was when, exactly?). His quick
dismissal – a wave – of any error
of thought or gloom of spirit;
the endless brilliant projects spilling out,
which might have been science, art, or some
new politics (one could make a proud career
from his leavings, while his praise became
the whole of one's morale) – I recognized
these, basked in them. Till gradually
or suddenly, I couldn't tell, I realized
and tried to avert the knowledge that
I had no idea who he was:
a god without portfolio, perhaps,
who shuttles, barely tolerated,
among the sofas of the other gods.

Modern Day Dangers of the Oregon Trail

Cassandra Lipp

In the July heat after a Got Junk truck carried off all our secondhand furniture, our remaining belongings departed in a moving pod, and my father-in-law started a squabble over Goldfish crackers rather than doing the more difficult task of bidding his son goodbye, my fiancé and I left our rented Kentucky townhome for our new house in Portland, Oregon.

Driving down the street we'd lived on for five years one last time, it was hard to believe the moment we'd worked toward that entire time had finally come. Long ago we realized our dreams were bigger than the town we grew up in—although as recent college grads, our wallets weren't. And so while our friends went out drinking and dancing and doing other things I'm told normal twentysomethings do, we spent all our time working. Me nannying while freelance writing and eventually a magazine editor, him red-eyed into the night producing YouTube videos about easter eggs in video games. When his YouTube success afforded us the ability to buy our first house, the tree-filled skies of the Pacific Northwest called us—home to as many writers as towering pines, and the epicenter of the American video game industry. The fact we had no family or friends there didn't matter. We set off on the 2,000-mile journey, just the two of us and the sack of Goldfish crackers my father-in-law swiped from an airplane.

The excitement of retracing the Oregon Trail was not lost on me. It was my favorite game growing up, making sure I had enough sacks of cornmeal and yards of muslin cloth before taking my fictional family from Missouri to Oregon. I didn't even know what muslin cloth was, and my family usually caught scarlet fever before I reached the end of the journey. During my angsty years, I discovered it was more fun to spend sleepovers with my friend naming our characters after people we didn't like and pushing them toward the deadly fates of the trail on purpose. My curmudgeon fourth-grade teacher's frostbite was rubbed with snow. The boy who teased us in class was fed poisonous berries. At least my rebellious phase never included drinking or smoking or actually feeding people poison berries.

Thankfully, my fiancé and I didn't have many dangers to worry about on the Oregon Trail in 2021—or so I thought. We drove through rain and shine past the Kentucky Bourbon Trail and the farmlands of Illinois. I sang "Meet me in St. Louis, Louis" dozens of times as the highway circled around the arch again and again. They were the only lyrics I remembered from the musical; my companion wished I remembered none. We ate burgers and shakes next to the burger-shaped car from *The Good Burger.* Once a prop from my favorite childhood movie, now scenery at a St. Louis burger joint. What would it be like to drive the rest of our trip in the burger car, smashing walls and speeding down the street like Kel Mitchell and Kenan Thompson once had? I suspect we'd be arrested long before reaching Portland.

We made our way through the endless green farmlands of Kansas. "Who waters all this grass?" I asked, and saw my answer in the form of helicopter-sized sprinklers. We passed villages of windmills powered by winds so strong my fiancé's arms were sore from keeping an iron grip on the steering wheel to prevent the car from swerving.

We couldn't resist the natural beauty of Colorado and stopped to stroll through a Fort Collins park. Tall grasses surrounded a pond, the Rockies playing peekaboo in the distance. How far should we walk the trail before going back to the car? Not far—we had 16 more hours to drive and wanted to keep an eye on the car, which held some of our most valuable possessions (not to mention Goldfish). The wildflowers and grasses we disappeared into were so lovely I didn't mind that the trail was taking us further from the car as it transformed from a gravel path to a boardwalk, that it was winding so much I was losing my sense of direction and the midday sun was growing hotter on our backs.

I was lost in awe of the wind swaying through the plants when I was interrupted by a scaly, black-and-brown spotted creature hissing at us. Those sharp fangs, that unmistakeable rattle—I'd seen this in a cutscene from *Oregon Trail.* In all the excitement of getting out of the car to stretch our legs, we missed the signs warning visitors about rattlesnakes. Did someone out there playing *Oregon Trail* hold a grudge against me?

I remembered enough from the game that I knew the safest method to get away from a rattlesnake. My fiancé had the same instinct, slowly walking backward until we were out of the rattlesnake's view and then sprinting like hell to the end of the path. We were safely out of the grass with no snakes in sight, but in the opposite direction of the car. There was no way we were going back on the path after finding out it was home to snakes. Our only option was to walk down the sidewalk surrounding the perimeter of the park until we reached the car, now a mile away. Had I known we were going to trek this far, I would have changed out of my flip-flops. And applied sunscreen.

Hearts still racing from the snake encounter, we got back to the car an hour later then made our way through the towering rocks of Wyoming, a state I'd never been to before, but learned the hard way that hurricane-strength winds blow through the fields. *I guess they don't call these the Wind Hills for nothing*, I thought, holding down my skirt with all my might to avoid giving other travelers at the rest stop a show. It was then that my fiancé told me my back was fire-engine red, with a sunburn so bad it left a handprint when he touched it. My fourth-grade teacher must have been getting back at me for her frostbite.

I knew I had to slather aloe vera lotion on my back as soon as possible before the sunburn began to sting, but I hadn't had the foresight to pack any. The rare highway exits we passed consisted of lone gas stations. The Wind Hills were gorgeous, but I longed to see a Walgreens. Would I have to resort to my *Oregon Trail* skills and ask people at each stop if they'd like to trade? *Please sir, will you trade your aloe vera lotion for 20 bags of Goldfish?* Or, I could play the role of Oregon Trail bandit and raid one of the many Amazon trucks along the highway.

It occurred to me that due to my unpreparedness, we were roughing it on the Oregon Trail just like the hundreds of thousands who crossed America in covered wagons. As the sky turned pink and the sun disappeared behind rocky cliffs and tumbleweeds, I felt a kinship with those who risked everything—snakebite, sunburn, and all—to build new lives out West. Just like us.

Vegetation Meditation
Karla Linn Merrifield

When viewed from a sturdy suspension bridge
above the Monteverde Cloud Forest canopy,
it is not the howlers who beguile me, but the leaves.
How ingenious are the leaves' green strategies,
a veritable spectrum of breathing green conceptions.
In a similar vein, I squint to note the myriad multitextures
of the leaves, squint to study the diversity of leaf-shapes,
come to prefer palmate, as in the sloth's cecropia.
One leaf, a mouthful, sustenance at the top
in a climax tree, before me a giant-sized botanical
of botanicals— I look, see from orchid
to tree fern to liana to master and champion:

The leaves live in the abundances of leafy kingdoms;
the leaves bid me step inside their stomata.

for Pamela Hesline

Growing Season—3 Haiku
Jennifer Overturf

A seedling sprouting
Green leaves from warm damp soil rise
Looking for the sun

Every basket full
We have been waiting all year
For summer's bounty

The frost is coming
Blight and pests have ravaged you
Every season ends.

The Scion of March Mountain

J. Paul Ross

A rusted bottle cap sits atop a mound of pine needles.

A gold-plated flask rests on the woodpile, gleaming in the alpine sun.

And a loaded .270 Winchester rifle sits against the lodge's front door.

It's unusually hot, even for late August, and the thin air tastes of bristle-cone, lodgepole, and ponderosa. Their aromas fill the mountain breeze and invade the reek of whiskey sweat pouring from John March's skin. Its stench oozes from his clothing and it's plastered his thinning grey hair to his forehead. He's tired, his breaths are heavy and he leans the rake on his narrow chest and stares at the blisters on his palms.

They're dark pink and split open, and with every movement of his fingers, a jolt of pain courses from his hands to his shoulders. He doesn't know when they formed or when they ruptured but he wishes he'd brought a pair of gloves. They would've saved him from wincing each time the rake caught on the rocky earth and they would've made the morning just a little bit easier. He could've worked faster, gotten more done, but he had no idea this sort of labor could be so hard. By nine, his forearms were cramping in knotted waves. By ten, his back was in spasms and by noon, he was exhausted. His knees are weak, he can barely stand and, wiping his brow, he glares at the twenty mounds it's taken him half a day to build.

Some close to two feet tall, they pepper the granular soil like anthills and extend from the wooden deck to the forest's edge. They're a desiccated brown and irregularly shaped, and they bristle with seedless pinecones, frail twigs, snapped branches and thin needles.

The land obviously hasn't been cleared in a long time and he's been trying to recall whether the caretaker quit, retired, or died. It's been awhile and he not only can't remember what happened to the man but he's also uncertain when he last saw him. Was it between his father's funeral and his uncle's lawsuit? Or was it when his second wife attempted to steal the land in the divorce? He knows the man was here when he had to rewrite his will after the summons from his niece's lawyers. In fact, they might've actually shared a glass of single malt that day, but he can't be sure because until this year, he hadn't visited this place in ages.

At twenty-five hundred feet below timberline and practically surrounded by the White River National Forest, the mountain was difficult to reach. It was a three-hour commute from the city over uneven roads and winding switchbacks and, besides the occasional hunting trip, he'd rarely thought of it. For at least a decade, it'd been nothing but a souvenir of a valueless past: a tax write-off, a number in a ledger, an asset tallied with all the others.

But then came recessions and quarterly disappointments, bad advice and unproductive investments, and it suddenly became something else.

It became collateral, a down payment on his future, his redemption, and his sole remaining hope.

The breeze rises and curls. It twists the corners of the sun-washed paper in his back pocket and drives splinters of light across the bottle cap a few feet away. Bent and dirt-covered, its logo has long since faded but he wonders if it's from the afternoon his cousins captured a chipmunk.

It was the summer before he started boarding school and they were laughing as they used a BB gun to shoot at it in a bucket. The tiny animal scampered around and around, chirping in panic until the two boys finally killed it and cut off its tail with a pocketknife.

They took turns wearing their trophy on their ball caps and John March unconsciously brushes the spot where his grandfather slapped him. He'd been trying to bury the animal when the old man discovered him and grabbed him by the scruff of his neck. There was a hateful scowl, a comment on weakness and then a loud strike. It echoed among the trees and ricocheted against outcroppings of stone. It made his ears ring and he scurried to the lodge to find his mother with tears clouding his vision. He whimpered and sniffled, and when he found her, still holding his right cheek, she put her soda bottle on the deck and struck him on the left one.

His bloodshot eyes return to his palms and the blister forming on the tender, pale skin between his right thumb and forefinger. It's swollen and ready to burst and he drops the rake and heads to his flask on the woodpile.

The stack is canted and pieces of lumber have rolled to the ground. Spider webs choke the triangular nooks and much of it has weathered to a soft gray. It seems smaller to him because when he was little, he used to spend hours climbing its massive bulk and using it to construct huge forts with . . .

He sneers.

It's been decades since *she's* crossed his mind and he's angry with himself at almost whispering her name and at remembering when they were last together.

They'd been arguing during their brother's memorial service. There was the smell of charring wood, the crack of pinesap and, the explosions of sparks from the fireplace had been accompanying her voice while it grew more insistent. She wanted to build a ski resort here but he kept telling her no. She fumed and yelled and claimed it was the *family's* mountain, not his.

But it was his. It was *his* birthright, *his* land just as it had been his father's, his grandfather's and his great-grandfather's.

Starting with an insignificant parcel taken from the Utes, they'd purchased, bargained and sued until they owned the whole peak from base to summit. For generations, it'd carried the family name and for generations, they'd held it and fought for it; they beat Teddy Roosevelt when he tried to take it. They thrashed FDR when he wanted to seize it for the WPA and they even withstood Reagan and the mining companies.

It would always be his no matter what his sister tried. When the judges dismissed her five court cases, it was his. When she was in the cancer ward, it was his and it was still his when they buried her in a cheap casket.

His sneer coils and he shifts his embittered glare toward the barren stone crests and shadowed hollows of the distant Continental Divide. Even from here, he can see the winds caressing the hills and valleys between his mountain and its slopes. They brush the rolling carpet of evergreens and patches of rust-colored beetle kill. They scour aspen groves with ivory bark and amber edged leaves. They glide below the midday sun, churn the dusty soil and he shakes his head and brings his grandfather's flask to his parched lips.

The 101 proof alcohol plunges into his stomach and he's about to cough when the winds change direction and a gust almost makes him stagger. The sweat from his brow evaporates in its hot blast. It bends treetops, scatters needles and listening to its hypnotic rustle sounding like the ocean's tide battering the surf, he thinks he hears his father's voice. There's the deliberate inhalation, the anticipatory pause and he cranes his neck.

He doesn't know what the lesson will be. Is it going to be a terse order, a lengthy criticism or merely a ploy to test if he's listening? Will his response evoke a gruff snort of approval or a testicle-shrinking frown? It was impossible to tell with his father but there was always a never-to-be-ignored point: a story of conquest, a parable on the importance of family, the need to win no matter what and, above all else, to never lose.

There's another gust, only more violent.

Then another one and another one after that.

He sighs.

He's been waiting for them and though they weren't supposed to come until sunset, he's glad they're here.

Already, his carefully organized mounds are fragmenting and he takes a final drink and empties the remaining whiskey onto the tallest pile. The alcohol splashes over the needles and twigs, and he drops the flask, retrieves his cigar lighter and removes the paper from his pocket.

He doesn't turn the wheel against the flint until the air stalls and the mountain is quiet. There's a spark, an ignition, and a stinging jolt. He doesn't wince, however. Instead, he brings the document he'd torn off the front gate to the fire and watches. The flame quickly incinerates the letters *IRS* and once it's consumed the words, *Notice of Seizure*, he lets it fall into the kindling. There's the scent of ash, of smoldering wood and, ignoring the wind's bellow, he collects his rifle, walks into his lodge and closes the door.

Rough-Cuts

Tyler Fisher

We would not call them knotholes.
No, far more than knots,
those vortices of woodgrains
on our walls
were sighing hurricanes
in pine
and wizened eyes
or eyelets in an archipelago of splintered isles
in a rough-sawn tide
where resin's undertow
so long ago
cut short the ripples of its amber flow
to map the whispered promises in wooden
portals,
portholes in the planks
where whorls of branches once had stretched their tips to punctuate
the skies.

Three Haiku

Robert Witmer

skin
brown and bruised –
the fruit within decays

exposed roots
the countless steps
of refugees

rising tide
she lifts her skirt
to wipe away a tear

When the Quiet Part is Said Loud

Kelley Swan

They crammed us out back, at the rear of the building. We waited under the shade of a metal roof on stilts where they'd squashed us onto a patch of pavement. Our own little refugee encampment. We were sandwiched in on one side by the parking lot, so the grills of sun-bleached cars stared back at us.

On the other side leered an empty daycare. Its playground baked in the heat. Swings hung listlessly, their frames set on artificial grass the most vibrant of greens, intent on giving nature the finger. A dented kitchen timer, plopped down on a table, ticked away one hour.

The facility door opened. A mountain lumbered toward us. I hugged the wall to avoid being plowed down by this stranger.

He laughed. My child. "Don't you know me?"

No. No, I didn't.

He reached out to fist bump me. "It happens."

With the pandemic, quarterly family visits on the taxpayers' dime had been suspended along with life. So we're all strangers here now, at this place where our home-state discards their neurologically disabled. They pay Florida to keep them, so they can forget them. Like prisons and the homeless, no one wanted our grown children contaminating their backyard.

The plastic Adirondack creaked under his weight as my son collapsed onto it. Headphones looped around his head, like some sort of Beats halo. They were plugged into the empty space that's nothing, and he was nodding in time to music only he could hear. His drooping mask had fallen under his nose.

"Fix the chin diaper," I said, just so he can ignore me.

The other families were clustered around their tables. One father cried, openly but noiselessly, facing off with the brick wall across from him. His wife twisted her hands together, over and over, as their son paced in a tight three-step pattern: heel, toe, pivot. Then he slapped his forehead, muttering to himself. Back and forth, he went. His mask was securely on, though.

A woman sat in a back corner by the dead potted mini palm. Her son was slumped in his wheelchair, thudding against it rhythmically, his arm twisted up only inches from her face. She was too young to be so worn. I wondered if she had other children. Maybe little ones, back at the two-star hotel we were all booked at, with grandma babysitting. She looked like she'd been trying to wield magic, turning this visit into a vacation with too much pool time, because she was glowing.

Her skin was burnt, that too-white tourist from up north painful kind of sunburnt. A perfect hot pink border encircled stark white sunglass patches around her eyes. Limp hair stuck to her skin, damp. Even her words seemed to cling to her as she steamed in the heat.

"So miserable." I must have said it out loud. My husband snorted, a small laugh, as he said, "Aren't we all, though."

Some more than others. But yes. We were.

She began to slap down photos onto the picnic table. Like flashcards of home, it was a recitation of here's your grandpa who died while you were gone, and slap! The new pets we have now you've never met, and double slap!

A photo fell to the ground. She reached down, in fluid motion, and saved it. Slap! The baby cousins born while you were away that you'll never know.

The son was agitated. Whining. He was now slamming himself back into his chair. His arm almost thwacked her in her sun-scorched face. I flinched for her.

They're all agitated, these clients, as they're called. Changes in schedules, visitors, they hip-checked them right off their balance. We were too much for them.

His whining grew louder. "When can I go home, why can't you just take me home."

Her lips curled in on themselves. Escaping, becoming the thinnest of lines, growing smaller and smaller until they were lost in a burnt backdrop.

"I just want to go home," he wailed.

The woman slammed her hands down on the wood. The flimsy table shook, scattering photos. Shocking him, and all of us, into muteness.

"You're never going home!" she shouted.

The son burst into tears.

A hush fell again and the weightiest of silences settled all around us as we sat and stared everywhere but at each other.

My son yanked off his headphones and laughed, too loud. I tried to shush him.

"What," he said, laughing again. "It's not like she's wrong."

Frigatebirds Soar for Weeks Over the Ocean Without Stopping

Kyle Potvin

Aviary of strangeness, O ancient seabird, your
beak, slender and hooked,
crooks its bill at me. Come.
Do you want to land in my hand,
enter my lonely cage?
Forked and fierce,
Genus Fregata, you
hang over me, your man-long wingspan a shade
in this scalding sky.
Jostle me madly to regurgitate what
keeps me anchored here.
Loosen my grip from this rail.
Make me fear I may
never fly
off this balcony.
People are meant to stay grounded, aren't they?
Quenched by their simple wants.
Rescue by bird is impossible yet
save me.
Take me to your thermals,
upstroke of deltoid,
vertical keel of
wonder soaring, soaring, without one wing flap.
X out expectations of what is wingless, solitary.
Yearning is all I want to feel riding on your feathered back.
Zillions of flower-birds around me: a flock, a fleet, a flotilla.

Jebediah

Ted Marcelo

I'd teach you when to fight and pray you'd never have to,
but if you ran home and said you won,
I guess that prayer's only half-true, and half broken Spanish, Jersey English
and the lightest dash of Greek,
'cause like our padre Jesús quien rested en el cielo at the telos
of the week, your cries dribbled holy water,
and whose first words outlined the second book of Kings,
which is a brief peek
of what happens when a Catholic's baby sings.
But I say cat-ho-lics like you can hear those hugging squibbles,
lowercased flat italics
by the weight of two cultures fighting to pay for steaks and salads every dinner,
money we didn't really have to dress the bride after
unprotected sex like a pair of sinners could make
you
of anything.

There are too many things I didn't get to say,

Like you can have that bowl of Cheerios to mark and cap your every day,
but when you're almost 30 you start to count its price,
and when they ask for your background,
they're not asking you that question twice;
ethnicity checks Hispanic, but you box race off as Other
cause you're not white-white,
quite Asian, and no one will call you brother,
and five-eight is a perfectly average height, not the universe sizing you unjustly,
I mean, tu viejo pulled some real surprises so you'll have to trust me.
Plus, I didn't have any of your goings-on mid-curly waves,
these eyes only trapped the light that your dusk-lit fires save,
to be caught again by this nose of ours,
that they might say is quite exotic.

You know, your blood's both more diverse than mine and capable to pass,
which I think's a bit ironic.
Which is to say, you'll be fine, but aren't defined by what might
please a woman. (Don't tell that to your mother).

Do you remember that park in Paterson, snow and litter covered,
where my dad sold his years in popsicles,
you called so ugly you'd never visit twice?
I'd think he'd tell you those were weekends he should've saved for us, we're not
what we sacrifice.
Which is not to say you won't have to work, and while
you'll find jobs in packing eggs last in paper, in cold calling for a commission,
while you claim your stake in this nation's wealth,
you'd be mistaken to let that chase or title replace your definitions
When you introduce yourself, it's not
'name
comma
company position,'
it's who you are by what you can't help but pursue,
too often that's confused for what we're paid to do.

I know I've only told you what you're missing
by way of what we're not,
but that's what I picked up without you.
Right now, that's all I got.

You could have had some questions of your own,
like where do these memories fit
in the space between flesh and bone?

Well, you know how you slept to the screams and cries,
but knew the love your mom and I could not share would still twist into knitted feathers
for one chance to hold you?

There are paths wound
from Time
when I've told you
how your birth was worth the cost of everything I've thought
myself before,
where I've handed you my pieces and you'd get to hand them down
once more.

Timber of the Gods: An Ancient Tree in a Care Center Parking Lot

Trista Cornelius

We're at the memory-care center visiting my dad. It's March 1st, 2021, and we're still doing window visits. The staff and residents have been vaccinated, but we have not. COVID19 still threatens us and the care center is still closed to indoor visits, so we stand outside my dad's bedroom window, shout through the two-inch opening, wave three dozen times, then leave after about a half an hour.

We do this once a week, every week. My child and I drive over an hour to pick up my mom and take her to the care center. I don't exactly enjoy this, but she and my dad have been married 61 years, and it seems like something I must do, even during these months of window visits which guarantee we won't be able to hear him talk if, by chance, his words are making sense. But it's rewarding to get him to smile. I hold an open black umbrella behind my mom, creating shade so she can see through the glare of the window. Otherwise, it's like a mirror. My right hand aches from the subtle writhing of the handle as gentle wind adds weight to the umbrella then threatens to lift it away.

In my left hand, I'm holding a pinecone. Well, we thought it was a pinecone at first. In the pristine driveway beside my dad's window, a giant tree looms beatifically. Tan cones stand upright at the end of branches with scales tightly coiled, not open like a pine or fir cone.

My octogenarian mother and first-grade child are both fascinated by these cones. Placating them, I pull a cone off a low branch on our way to my dad's window where they both temporarily lose interest, which leaves me holding the cone in my left hand, harnessing the umbrella with my right. I squint through the shiny window only to discover my dad is bald. Dementia has changed a lot of things about my dad, but not his hair.

For at least twenty years now, he's had silky, shiny, downright shimmering, white hair. You can find him in any crowd because his head gleams. It's striking and beautiful, but also something I'm so used to seeing, I only know it's unique because people frequently point it out. But in all our 48 years together, I have never seen him bald. We don't know why the caretakers have shaved his head because we can't hear them through the window and mask and face shield, but my dad's hair is shaved all the way off for whatever reason.

He looks pretty good. I'm not as shocked as I would have thought I'd be. He has a nice shaped head. I'm more bothered by his yellow and brown teeth. No matter how diligent and skilled his caretakers are, there's only so much other people can do for your teeth. He just doesn't know what a toothbrush is anymore. Sometimes he doesn't know what a fork is for, so I don't hold any blame.

The first grader jumps around and pretends to appear magically underneath the umbrella. The sun beams on my left hand still holding the cone when I suddenly feel and hear a "pop." A subtle shock to my palm. I look down and one scale of this tightly closed cone has spread out.

I'm amazed and try to tell my mom and child, but one is busy chasing the wind and the other is saying "What's that? I can't hear you," as she leans far over the hedge toward her own reflection. I marvel at this thing in my hand, living out its life right here in my palm.

I eventually turn back toward the window when it happens a second time, "pop," and another scale has pushed open. There's something about the confidence of this cone, the way it follows its own genetic timing, maybe sensing the heat of my palm, and beginning its next stage of existence. I feel elated. Full of reassurance. Grateful for this cone in my hand.

We walk back to my car. My child and mother play with the sticky sap from the cone and discover that hand sanitizer removes it, which of course we smother our hands in once we get back to the car, even though we've touched nothing but the tree and our umbrella because we're more than a year into the pandemic, and frankly, I don't know if I'll ever stop using hand sanitizer every time I transition from one place to another.

I cheer up when the alpine tree scent cuts through the caustic hand sanitizer smell.

The following week when we pick up my mom for our window visit, a sturdy booklet titled "Trees to Know in Oregon" published by Oregon State College (now Oregon State University) in 1957 sits out on the counter. According to this book our tree is a true cedar, native only to the Old World.

"Few people are able to distinguish Deodar from the Atlas cedar," the book tells us. Which is why I put a small, plastic ruler into my purse before we leave for the care center. This time, our visit is short. My dad's eyes seem unable to focus further than a few feet in front of him. He stares just past his knees. If he sees us at all, his compressed sense of distance must make us look like blurry trees swaying in the wind.

The ruler in my pocket gives us a convenient distraction. Measuring the needles on our tree becomes the reason we walk away from my dad's window after only a few minutes, bypassing guilt and worry with curiosity and science.

We measure the needles twice. Deodar needles are one-to-two inches long, Atlas needles are shorter. I am thrilled to know this is a Deodar cedar, that we're some of the "few people" let in on the secret of this ancient tree, a tree so sacred in Hinduism that its name means "timber of the gods" in Sanskrit.

Later, I learn that the scales on the cone of the Deodar cedar break away while the cone is still attached to the tree. What finally falls from the tree is just the central spike that the scales once clung to so tightly. I was lucky to have reached a mature cone to pluck from a low branch, and I was right to marvel at its opening in my hand.

On April 21st, three weeks after picking the cedar cone, we bring my mom for our usual weekly visit. This time, my dad is allowed to sit outside with us. This is the first time in a year that I've seen him without shining glass between us. His hair has grown back a half-inch or so. It takes a few of us to help him sit down. He's not only somewhat weak, he's confused. He doesn't seem to see, or maybe doesn't recognize, the bench. He says "Here? Here?" My child climbs through the bushes nearby, and I say something to him about not messing up the bark dust. I hear my dad's voice, but assume it's gibberish until I hear my mom giggling. She repeats what he said "When does dust bark?" and my dad starts to chuckle. It's not until the seven-year-old starts to laugh that I finally get the joke, that I finally realize I can't completely dismiss my dad as "gone." He still hears us. He can still sometimes sort of talk. He's still funny. And, in spite of the dwindling strength and agility of his body, his shimmering hair is growing back thick and lush. I can't help but wonder why. Why does his hair grow back so strong when more vital parts of him fade? This makes me think of the deodar cedar.

I make an excuse to leave my parents on the bench so I can walk around the building and check on our tree. A few dark brown scales collect near the curb. They look like moth wings. Otherwise, there's no sign of the tree's off-spring—seeds that can take 45 years for the tree to be ready to produce, and then bear only once every three years or so. I wonder if there will be cones next year. Then I wonder if I'll be here in this parking lot next year. Will my dad still be here? Will he still be alive? Is he dying now, or is he still living? I don't know the difference anymore.

I admire the Deodar's ever-present existence over so many generations of humans living under it. It continues to live out its life exactly as it…as it knows how to do? It must have adapted over all these years, made adjustments, but even so, I don't sense any hesitation or self doubt from this cone. It is what it's always been. It knows exactly what it's doing. Or better yet, it knows nothing: it simply responds to the seasons, the elements, its life stages. The tree is amazingly huge yet so easy to pass by without noticing. Until it comes to life in the palm of your hand.

Went to See the Doctor

Arthur Crummer

She seemed too young,
rolled up sleeve, pumped the cuff.

This morning, I was 14, worked the garden,
humming *Shady Grove*,
broke for lunch, felt 41, took a nap,

nothing wrong with that. Painted
porch rail, walked dog, foggy woods.

I was 52 driving to this appointment.
Where's the cheery family doc I saw back when
who listened to my answers, shook my little hand?

Now she stares at her computer, reads questions
from a decision tree. I answer, time slows.

Took in my computer yesterday,
technician looked about 12 years old.

Something about mother board…
might need ablation…can't remember.

Feeling dizzy, tilt back, exam table,
songs in my head: *Blue Christmas, Elmer's Tune, Stardust,
Time Changes Everything, Brother Can You Spare a Dime?*

Don Schlitz, Willie Nelson, Kris Kristofferson, Hoagie
Carmichael curl up beside me.
Yip Harburg whispers in my ear,
*where is the star that shone so bright,
ages ago, last night?*

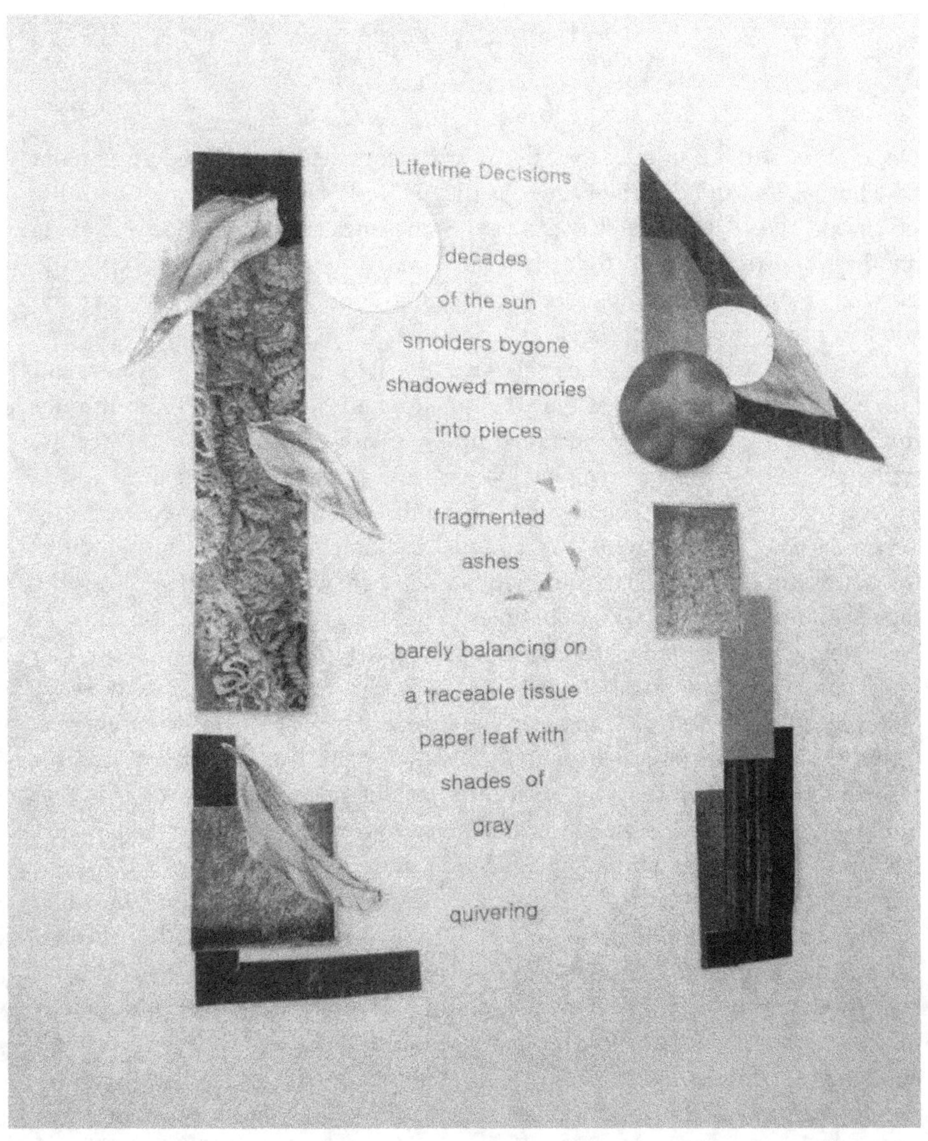

Lifetime Decisions
Roberta Pearla

Too Much With Us

Diane LeBlanc

On a humid afternoon in early August, my last defense is to stand among the rose bushes and remove the beetles as they land. It's not a perfect system. If I pinch one before it settles, it flies away. Sometimes my groping for one alerts another, and one or both fly away. But I measure steady progress with the growing number of shining bodies dragging spurs and claws through the soapy water in my plastic margarine container.

Japanese beetles are fierce this year. In the mid-day heat they descend like Hitchcock's birds except they are smaller and quieter, interested in only my roses. An early spring prompted grubs to rise from their winter depths, feed on lush roots, transform into pupae, and emerge as adult beetles. Although this summer has been Minnesota's third driest season on record, a few neighbors and I persist with our gardens. By late July, my hardy red shrub roses, the workhorses of past summer color, are chewed to the stem, blossoms ragged and buds hollow with bore holes.

Nearby lawns had sprouted Bag-a-Bug deterrents in early July. The green and white hourglass-shaped bags dangling from wire stakes were so colorful and inviting that I thought they were a new trend in hummingbird feeders. I left town for vacation before knowing the truth. By the time I returned, the bags were the sagging focal points of surrounding yards. My dog and I passed one yard whose entire perimeter was lined with bags, each equipped with a plastic chute and a 2-inch round lure. Apparently, the scent mimics beetle pheromones. Although the lures contain oils from the same spices I use to mull cider, the air around the yard smelled faintly of urinal cakes. One morning, I couldn't help myself. I bent over and peeked into a bag. At least two cups of beetles were churning and crawling over one another in slow motion. Whatever chemicals seduced them into the bag weren't enough to kill them.

I start to question my impulse to save my roses. The first blossoms in early June were magnificent. Drivers passing the house slowed down when I was outside, opened a window, and called out, "Beautiful!" and "Such great color!" I tended them daily, snipping away bald hips after petals fell. Blossoms are fragile as they pass. One brush of my hand or the scissors and petals drop like unglued pages. Always, after the first blossoms have gone by, I feel a wave of grief. Summer is slipping away, and I haven't done enough during these precious long days. But as I bend closer, looking to cut away dead growth, I see tightly wrapped maroon leaves sprouting from toughened stems. New growth will stretch into leafy shoots and host the next burst of blossoms.

***

I research solutions to my beetle problem. Plucking and dropping individual beetles into a mix of Ivory soap and water is short-sighted. No matter how many I eliminate, more come to clump and glisten in the mid-day heat. One gardening blog suggests treating the lawn with grub killer to stop the beetles at their source. With dogs and a nearby pond, I avoid lawn chemicals. I consider Bag-A-Bug but read that they actually may attract the pests. My husband buys one while I'm still debating consequences. I plant it 30 feet from the garden, as instructed, to see what happens. After two days, I'm convinced our front yard is the epicenter of the invasion.

I also search for a definitive reason not to destroy the beetles. When I Google "Benefits of Japanese Beetles," I find only descriptions of their destructive patterns, their robust mating, and, in one blog, their only redeeming quality: chickens love to snack on them. I imagine friends with chickens politely declining offers from do-gooders approaching the gate with their green and white sacks of groggy bugs. "No thanks, we have our own." The chickens are probably sick of beetles by now. That's what happens when you overdo an extraordinary snack.

***

I move through the garden like a robot. Two minutes on one bush, two minutes on the next. Round and round I go, talking myself out of any remaining hope to save my roses. I remove every beetle in sight, then snap the lid on my brown soup of beetles and soap. August days have a rhythm. Write, work in the yard, ride my bike. Today I pedal on trails through restored prairie where bloom and decay live together, sometimes on the same plant. Beside tight green pods, plump with silk and seed, milkweed leaves curl stippled with yellow aphids. On a single sumac branch, some leaves burn early red while others wither to brown from heat and drought. I return home after an hour to find new beetles glinting on the wreckage of the last big feed. But I'm done for another day.

***

Japanese beetles have natural predators. Possums and raccoons eat the grubs. But they tear up grass to get them. Do I want to trade one problem for another? Another predator, the cardinal, inspires a salvation myth. I imagine the first lone cardinal visiting to nibble on a few grubs. Then another comes to the feast. And another. Soon my front yard would teem with pecking cardinals. But this hasn't been a good year for birds. A haze of smoke from Canadian wildfires has been hanging over southern Minnesota for weeks. Fires in much of the West, too, are displacing and killing birds. On a U.S. Forest Service bird atlas, southern Minnesota is vibrant blue, reflecting high recorded observations, while the Northwest is a pale yellow landscape of low observations, extinction only a matter of time.

***

The longer I patrol the roses, the more closely I observe my garden's ecosystem. Forced from the roses, the beetles start feeding on the cleome, those gangly wild roses that seed themselves every year. I consider letting the beetles have the blossoms since the seed pods are already reaching outward like delicate green fingers. But what would I be feeding? Female beetles mate and lay eggs every day or two. In her lifetime, a month or six weeks at most, a female will lay up to five dozen eggs. If I give her the cleome blossoms, I'm aiding and abetting. Even worse, the bees are competing with the beetles for blossom time. No blossom, no pollen, no bees.

The beetles and I meet every day for a week until a brief afternoon storm interrupts my vigil. Wind and rain shake twigs and dead leaves into the streets. By evening, the air is less humid and smoky. I return to the garden hoping the storm has rinsed away the pests. On the way, I pull my container of soapy water and plucked beetles from its nook in the hedge, just in case. The roses look plump with rain. Fully fleshed leaves are opening on bold maroon stalks. Then I see it. A centimeter spot on a tight new bud is the copper flash of a burrowing pest. I squeeze the beetle from the bud like a fat sliver and drop it into the suds.

Rationally I know that more than rain is required to eliminate an invasive species. Japanese beetles arrived in the United States in the early 20th century, still grubs burrowed in the soil packed around imported irises. Their native habitat had natural population control, including predators and the absence of suburban lawns. As with zebra mussels and buckthorn in Minnesota, individual removal and diligent environmental hygiene have proven most effective. But species migrate in ways humans don't always predict. On a nearby park path, now that I'm attentive, I notice skeletonized leaves on wild grape vines and on willow leaves. I almost cheer for the beetles destroying these invasive plants, but there's no winner here.

***

I'm a creature of cycles, cicada rhythms, and seasonal eating. But lately, once-predictable seasons and rituals are slipping away. Changes aren't sudden, like rose petals dropping at a touch. At the local farmers market in mid-August, a farmer tells me his zucchini is done for the year. I wonder how I'll bake zucchini bread with local ingredients in mid-September to continue the tradition of mailing a loaf to my nephew in Vermont. The ritual connects us and keeps intact my role as the earthy aunt who honors each solstice with a homemade gift. Is it even possible to recalibrate my internal calendar to align with an evolving environment?

Beetle season should have passed by now. Before I knew what kind of summer lay ahead, I planted a half-dozen marigolds in front of the roses. I imagined a blast of orange deepening into October beside the crimson mums. Later I learned that Japanese beetles go first for marigolds. Not true. The sacrificial annuals are going strong while the roses recede. I linger in the garden long enough to perfect my killing technique. I pinch a cluster of beetle-heavy buds from behind with my thumb and forefinger, cupping my other fingers to prevent escape, then rub gently. Six to eight beetles drop into the soapy water. If a petal or bud drops with them, they cling to it. I stop watching the tumbling and floating. I tell myself what I want to be true. A few blossoms are better than none. The bees need me. And this ritual is still about my roses and the little plot I defend.

Sign

HC Hsu (許翔程)

Do
Not
Please do not
Love

Please
Wash hands
Before and after
Use

There
Is possibility
Of contamination
Of love-borne illness*

What
Lovely terminal terminology
Love
Borne
Bred
Bit

With a sweet and slightly burnt aftertaste
Or the stench of putrid rotten flesh
Buzzing about
In a ballad of death

Love
Is a dirty puddle next to a food stall by the gutter

Cholera
In the time of
Love

Please
Rest in peace
After use

*Acquired immune deficiency syndrome, or AIDS, is translated in Chinese as 愛滋病 [aizibing], literally 'love-borne disease'.

標記

許翔程

不
請不要
愛

請
前後
洗手

會
有愛
滋的病

多
美的名詞醫學
愛
所滋生
所滋潤
的滋味

是
一種微焦的甘甜
或者肉糜的腥臭
縈繞著死亡
的華爾滋

愛
是臭水溝旁路邊攤潑出去的一攤髒水

霍亂
在愛之
時

便後請
順變

When Titans Collide
(A Tete-a-tete between Two Celebrated Cerebrums)

Michael Nethercott

Who among us has not fantasized about being a fly on the wall at some momentous past event? This fly, of course, would need to be an historically aware one so as to know that the scene being observed was worth investing a chunk of one's (appallingly scant) month-long lifespan upon. And most fortunate, indeed, would be the presence of pen and paper and, ideally, the ability of the fly to take shorthand.

We possess such a fly in the anonymous scribe who witnessed the following meeting between Karl Marx and Sigmund Freud. Although the authenticity of this recently discovered account is, at best, foggy and unverifiable, it should by no means be lumped in with such falsified tomes as the Hitler diaries or those disreputable love letters between John Wilkes Booth and Mary Todd Lincoln. No, this is the real McCoy.

Marx and Freud, those two world-class thinkers, met in Vienna in the fall of 1863 at the home of mutual friends. At this time, Marx, age 45, had already established himself as one of the prominent architects of Revolutionary Proletarian Socialism. For his own part, Freud, age 7, had established himself as an individual who no longer wet the bed. Secure in their respective triumphs, the two encountered one another for the first time—Freud in his capacity as a precocious tot requiring an hour's babysitting; Marx as graying, grumbly "Uncle Karlie." We are indebted to the unknown third party who jotted down this endearing exchange.

\# \# \#

KARL: I've been asked by your mother to read to you from this volume of nursery rhymes. I will comply.

SIGMUND: I'm too old for such childishness.

KARL: Nonetheless, you will listen. You may well find the recitation instructive. Now, to begin: *Little Jack Horner...* Ah, do you see how, from the onset, this individual has been diminished and trivialized by the juggernaut of capitalism? He is dismissed as being Little Jack, as if he exists only as a tiny fleck in a faceless labor force. Do you see this?

SIGMUND: I think that Jack is little because he's convinced himself that he's little. He apparently suffers from some manner of nervous disorder.

KARL: Perhaps, but not likely. Let us move on: *Little Jack Horner sat in a corner...* His placement in the corner suggests a punitive action. Possibly, Comrade Horner is being punished for encouraging the masses to toss off the shackles of a commodities-based oligarchy.

SIGMUND: Or maybe he's in the corner because he is trying to face his anxieties. It's an obvious attempt to explore the shadowy recesses which lie beneath his conscious mind.

KARL: I think, my boy, you are drifting astray of the rhyme's core meaning. We continue: *Eating a Christmas pie...* This line obviously refers to the mandated consumption of religious iconology. Jack is being force-fed what I might label the opiate pie of the people.

SIGMUND: I disagree. I think eating Christmas pie represents the search for an effective treatment for Jack's disorder. Jack wishes to have his anxieties probed so that he can enjoy a big flavorful reward filled with the fruits of successful analysis.

KARL: You say you're only seven?

SIGMUND: Seven and a half.

KARL: Anyway... *He put in his thumb...* The thumb unquestionably stands for a worker-student alliance. Those who have for so long been under the thumb of capitalism now rise up to grind down their oppressors. You, no doubt, have a different interpretation.

SIGMUND: I think when it says his thumb it really means his pee-wee.

KARL: Good heavens! Why would you think *that*?

SIGMUND: I think a lot of things really mean pee-wee.

KARL: Uh, well, let's get this over with, shall we? *And pulled out a plum...* Meaning the triumph of the Socialist ideal.

SIGMUND: Meaning the triumph of the ego.

KARL: Whatever. *And said, What a good boy am I!* The proletariat celebrates its successful revolution.

SIGMUND: Or, rather, Jack is finally cured.

KARL: Enough of this, I think. Why don't you be a good lad and tell me where they keep the strong spirits around here.

SIGMUND: But when will Mama be back? Where's my Mama? Oh, where's my gorgeous Mama?

Thus ends the chronicle.

Freezer Burn

Hannah Marshall

I'd freeze my eggs if I caught any glints
Of guts in my blood. Far too strange, the quince
Preserves turn in the fridge before I muster
The pluck to spread them on toast. Poor culled cluster,
My cells behind a Lean Cuisine. I wince
At travel plans, disappear into chintz
Curtains at social gatherings, convince
Myself I needn't shop. I'd filibuster!
I'd freeze,

Faced with man's near extinction, or a prince
In search of heirs. There's a good reason hints
Of snow close me indoors; even a duster
Shake's worth could hypnotize me with its luster.
Tired, I'd lay at the end of my prints.
I'd freeze.

Feliz Cumpleaño

Ashley Guadamuz

they cheer into my   ears   they my estranged biological family close to
my shoulders   kissing   my   young red cheeks as their rum infused
bodies leak into my nose   they wrap someone's black bandana around
my straight hair they cover my   small face and make me blind   I
can't see where mi   mamá went   and I feel I feel the wooden stick
tossed into my hands and it's too heavy   for my sweaty palms but they
want me to hit the   hit the piñata   *dale dale* they cheer

I feel   dewy droplets   of erratic afternoon rain coming down and my
shorts don't keep me safe and my chills grow and I can't see where mi
papá went   and I   feel dizzy but they keep cheering me they keep saying
I'm ripe and I can still play   and I know they are fueled with   Flor de
Caña and that's why they are lusting   for the coconut   for the guava
candy   inside   but I don't want to hit rainbow cardboard I want to
climb the rain of Managua   break   the lock along the gloomy clouds
keeping my ancestors safe

I want to be with them   listen to their stories wear what they wear
cover my body in clean cotton dresses and straw hats like them I want to
hear

niña, you're safe here.

Pipkin

Robert Sachs

In the evenings after work, Lawrence Pipkin, thirty, takes regular and solitary walks around his north side Chicago neighborhood. He's what Baudelaire might have called "a botanist of the sidewalk." It's a two-mile loop from his parent's three-bedroom apartment on Carmen Avenue. His course never varies, no matter what the season, no matter what the weather, and because he traces the same path year after year, he notices things others don't. Now, as he crosses the small bridge near his apartment, he notices a body floating face down in the drainage canal.

He'd had a bad day at work. His boss in the accounting department of Goldblatt's yelled at him for not being able to find a file. "What the hell good are you, Pipkin?" the boss had bellowed, loud enough for everyone to hear. Pipkin wanted to yell back, but he needed the job and so remained silent.

Looking at the body now, he wonders if it is someone he knows? Not likely, he concludes. His first impulse is to run back to his parents' apartment—that's how he thinks of it; not his apartment, but his parents'—and call the police. But he'll be obliged to wait on the bridge for them to come. They'll ask questions. Who knows how long it might take? He decides instead to continue walking.

He passes the barbershop on Kedzie Avenue just as Herman Cogan looks up from a magazine. Pipkin nods. Cogan waves. There was a time, in high school and before, when they were good friends. They graduated together in '46 Cogan stayed in the city for college while Pipkin went downstate. Of the two of them, the smart money was on Pipkin. He was the more serious student. He was accepted at Northwestern University School of Law. His failure to pass the bar after graduating from law school was a surprise and a *shanda.* Word of it had filtered feverishly through the neighborhood. People called his parents to express their sympathies. It was as if a child had died. And if that wasn't bad enough, his decision not to take the test a second time left friends and acquaintances perplexed. It's not unusual to miss the mark the first time. But the vast majority of people who take the exam a second time, pass. So why did Pipkin decide against re-taking it?

Cogan's mother, who has an opinion on most things, thinks it has to do with Pipkin's fear of failure. True, there is no shame in flunking the bar exam the first time. But on the off chance he flunks it a second, judgment would be swift and irrevocable. People would avert their eyes when passing him. So rather than chance it, Cogan's mother concludes, Pipkin withdrew. Pipkin will tell you he simply grew disenchanted with the law. It no longer held his interest. So he looked elsewhere. All of this history is contained in the nod Pipkin and Cogan share. He decides to stop and tell Cogan about the body.

Pipkin puts his head in the door of the barbershop. "Crossing the bridge this evening, I saw a body floating in the canal," he says.

"A body," Cogan says. "Ha. Probably just shadows, Larry."

Pipkin nods. "Could be."

He dips into Rosenblum's candy store. As always, Mr. Rosenblum is behind the counter. He was there when Pipkin was a youngster, and he is there now. "Lawrence, my boy. Good to see you. Baby Ruth, right?"

"Right, Mr. Rosenblum. How is Howie?"

Howard Rosenblum is the bright light in Mr. Rosenblum's life. He had gone to law school with Pipkin, graduating in the bottom half of his class. He passed the bar on the first try. Mr. Rosenblum's second cousin, a precinct captain and old friend of the mayor, put in a good word, and Howard got a clerkship with a federal district court judge. He's now a third-year associate at a silk-stocking law firm in the Loop. Their first Jew.

"Works like a dog," Mr. Rosenblum says. "Never a day off. Sometimes he sleeps at the office. They tell him what to wear, what to eat. This is a life?"

"He'll do fine," Pipkin says.

Mr. Rosenblum nods. "It's good to see you, Lawrence. Still making the rounds?"

"Somebody's got to do it," he says. He hesitates, wondering if he should mention the body floating in the drainage canal. He decides to go ahead: "Crossing the drainage canal bridge this evening? I thought I saw a body."

"Oy, yoi yoi, a body," moans Mr. Rosenblum. "You're sure it wasn't rocks or some cardboard thing kids threw in?"

"I'll take another look on the way back."

He drops the unopened candy bar in a garbage bin as soon as he leaves the store. When he was a child, he often stole candy bars from Mr. Rosenblum. They called it hocking back then, so it sounded less reprehensible. But it gnawed at Pipkin's conscience, so as an adult, he makes it a practice to stop in each day and purchase a candy bar. Occasionally he eats them. More often than not, he discards them.

Coming toward him in a wooden wheelchair is Abe Kronthal. He's got a small black and white cat in his lap. "Larry, how are you," the man shouts.

"Fine, Mr. Kronthal. Couldn't be better. Where are you headed?"

"Drug store."

"Medicine for the cat?"

"Very funny. And your mom and dad, how are they?"

"Everything's good."

Kronthal is about Pipkin's father's age. He used to run a hat shop on Maxwell Street. One day a guy came in with a gun and demanded all the money in the cash register. Kronthal refused, and the guy shot him in both legs. Pop. Pop. They thought he wouldn't live, but he did. They thought he wouldn't walk, and they were right. The gunman was never caught. Kronthal gets around pretty well in his chair. He hires a guy to carry him up to his apartment and down.

Pipkin scratches the cat behind its ear. "I heard there was a body floating in the drainage canal this evening," he says.

"I once saw a teenager throw a bicycle off the bridge into the canal. Sure it wasn't a bicycle?"

"Could be. Take care of yourself, Mr. Kronthal."

Passing the Hot Dog Palace, he sees Irv Stein and his brother Sid cleaning up. Irv served in the navy during the war and has a tattoo on his forearm. Neither are married. Pipkin knocks lightly on the window. Irv waves him in. The brothers seem to be doing well. There's talk of them opening another shop on the North Shore. Pipkin thinks it would be fun owning a restaurant. Right out of law school, he had an idea for one: a kosher deli.

"There aren't enough kosher delis?" his father asked. "Save your money. Get a regular job, and you'll be fine. A businessman you're not."

His father was probably right, but Pipkin wonders how things would have worked out if his father had encouraged him. "Woulda, coulda, shoulda," he says to himself.

"Have a dog, Larry. On the house," Sid says.

"I'll pass," Pipkin says. "But thanks. Just finished dinner. Crossing the drainage canal a while ago, I saw something floating in it. A body, perhaps. Maybe something else."

"Face up or face down?" Irv asks.

"Face down."

"Ever wonder why bodies always float face down? Is it a center of gravity thing?"

The roller-skating rink across the street reminds Pipkin of Sandra. He met her at an Alaska statehood party in January. They rubbed noses in a cardboard igloo and started dating. He took her to the rink on a Saturday night. He slipped on the ice and fell on his butt. There was some snickering. After that, she didn't seem interested in him.

He buys the evening paper at the elevated train station and walks up to the boy's club. A group of six boys are talking to a policeman. "Anything wrong, officer?" Pipkin asks.

"We had a report of a body floating in the drainage canal. Just wondering if these kids might have seen something." Pipkin tips his cap and moves on.

As he approaches the synagogue—the one where seventeen years earlier he became a bar mitzvah—he wonders if he should have told the police about seeing the body. He concludes that since the police already know about it, there is no sense getting involved.

The high school, a block long, is foreboding at night. There are no lights either in the front or the back. Pipkin feels it's a perfect place to be mugged. As always, he quickens his pace as he skirts around the back of the school toward the drainage canal.

On the bridge once more, Pipkin looks over the side. The body, if that's what it was, is gone. Was it the current? Did the police drag it out? If it was really there, he knows there will be an article about it in the paper.

But what if there isn't? What if the body has sunk to the bottom? Worse yet, he thinks, what if there never was a body? Can it have been his imagination? Was he wishing it was his bellowing boss? He stays awake through the night until around five when the sky brightens, and he hears the thud of the newspaper landing at the front door of the apartment building. He runs quickly down the stairs, hoping to find something, anything about the body he saw floating face down in the drainage canal.

Nothing. Maybe it was too soon, Pipkin tells himself. He'll check the afternoon paper. When he gets to work, he sees that his boss is not in his office. Perhaps he took the day off. Perhaps, he thinks, that was him in the canal. At lunchtime, he runs to the newsstand just outside the department store. He buys a paper and rifles through it. This time, he sees a small article about an unidentified body found in the drainage canal. So it's true! It wasn't a shadow, it wasn't a bicycle or a box. It was a body. He's too agitated to eat lunch and heads back to the office. As he gets off the elevator on the seventh floor, his boss yells out: "Pipkin, get in here."

Pipkin's face reddens, and he feels somewhat ashamed that his immediate thought is not, "Thank God it wasn't him."

Aubade

Olaitan Humble

first a girl becomes a quantum particle doing
jumping jacks in Balmer series/ then we say

the girl is invisible because a rivulet
of benediction flows in her umbworld

she tries fitting herself into a model of utopia
mornings pour into the day like molten gold

suckled from the sun/ like Klein bottles
denuded from their disorientation

she is driven/ driven by her therapist's
addiction to alprazolam & times

she plants a boll of torment
in her own garden

driven/ driven by her friend's ability
to swim while she drowns

drowning in tears of yesteryear
& the gas that fills the air

when her mother cuts onions
now she is stuck/ stuck in a limbo

& an endless perambulation
of penrose stairs/ like vectors

in Hilbert space she is trapped as
a placeholder/ driven by the days of yore

a staccato of sonic booms forces the girl
out of utopia then we say amen to living

in seclusion/ we say: dear lord if we are
to die let it be on our birthday

& should our body be cut to pieces
open a breach & thrust us into afterlife

as if to save Alfonsina Storni from drowning
or to say: fender-bender cannot kill doppelgangers

Raggatus

James Hancock

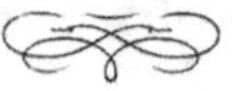

They bought a cat to kill the rats
That were living on the farm,
But the cat just sat and watched the rats
As they scurried about the barn.

As she slept most days in a loft of hay
The rats would brave a dance,
On the wooden loft, next to puss,
They danced the merry Raggatus.

Sixteen rats in a line,
Their tapping feet all in time,
And their nodding heads, a sight sublime,
The Raggatus.

Every day they teased the cat,
And danced the Raggatus behind her back.
Sliding feet, so quiet, so soft,
They jigged their jig across the loft,
The sleeping cat they mocked and scoffed,
The Raggatus. The Raggatus.

On the seventh day, she left her hay
And gave a wicked grin,
The cat had a plan, a devious plan,
And the rats would fall right in.

When exhausted rats were fast asleep
The cat had found a barrel deep,
Water-filled it without a peep,
Then returned to her straw pile heap.
And she slept.
Or so it seemed.

An hour passed, the sun grew heavy,
The rats emerged once more,
They climbed the loft and found their place
Upon the wooden floor.
And as the Raggatus began,
The cat triggered her dark plan.
With a fast claw, the wooden floor
Suddenly became no more,
A latch to the hatch of the dancing patch
Proved it was the loft's trapdoor.
To the rats' surprise the dance was stopped.
A twelve-foot drop, into water they plopped.

Thrashing and splashing
The rats began to drown,
The cat just smiled from up above.
The rats' last sight, her looking down,
And then silence.

Sixteen bloated, lifeless-floated,
While the cat gloated.

Clever puss,
No more dance of Raggatus.

Antifreeze

Laurie Easter

It's January 5th, and I'm on my way to town for the first time since Christmas. I've been holed up in my tiny off-grid cabin with my daughter and three-year-old grandson, all ill with the flu for the past ten days. On New Year's Day, I collapsed in the outhouse. I felt a shadow of darkness sweeping across my vision, so I put my head down between my legs, but the shadow took me anyway. I woke up frozen on the cedar-plank floor, unsure how long I had been lying there. Long enough for the January chill to seep into my bones. Not a great start for a new year—passed out cold above a heaping pile of shit. I wondered, then, if it was a metaphor for what was to come. But maybe the metaphor applies to what had already transpired and reflects how I'm coping? I feel stuck in a negative vortex. As I'm driving to town, I realize it's the nine-month anniversary of my husband's death.

Since his death, the 5th of each month has been significantly on my radar. Something I sit with, honor in silence, staring into the trees or up at the sky, allowing the weight of absence to consume me. "Be here now" was his favorite phrase. But he is not here now; I am, and the fact that I didn't realize the significance of the date until late in the day alarms me and I wonder, *am I already beginning to forget?*

My brain is struggling to regain its acuity due to illness. Yet my clarity of thought has been on hiatus much longer. I suffer from "Grief Brain," a response to the traumatic loss of a loved one, which causes the limbic system—the "primitive" part of the brain responsible for emotions, survival instincts, and memories—to go into overdrive. The brain perceives the traumatic loss as a threat to survival. As a result of the stress, the body releases an onslaught of hormones like cortisol that ratchet up the fear center of the brain, the amygdala, which stimulates the fight, flight, or freeze response. For nine months, I have been firmly planted in this raw, heightened emotional state of the body rather than an analytical or rational one. I mark my husband's death—first in days, then weeks, and now months. Time passes while I remain stationary in my grief.

In town, I go to Bi-Mart, an employee-owned, Pacific Northwest retail chain that offers one-stop shopping and allows me to get everything on my list while exerting the least amount of physical energy possible. I gather toilet paper, three boxes of Puffs tissues, a pack of fire starters, C and AAA batteries, razor cartridges, a new toothbrush, and toothpaste. Last on the list is antifreeze.

I once read a cheap supermarket mystery in which neighborhood dogs were being poisoned. The culprit used antifreeze. Ethylene glycol, the main ingredient, is lethal. Dogs are attracted to the sweet taste of antifreeze and if ingested—even as little as a tablespoon—it can be fatal. This knowledge stuck with me. And later, as the wife of an auto mechanic who worked from home with toxic chemicals, I worried about an accidental fatality of one of our pets.

As I stand in the automotive aisle looking at the antifreeze, a woman salesclerk at least ten years older than my fifty-two years rounds the corner and passes. She says, "Let me know if I can help you with anything."

There are two choices of antifreeze: full strength and diluted. I've never heard of diluted, and wonder, *is antifreeze supposed to be diluted?* I say to the clerk, "I notice this is diluted…"

She says, "That's just for convenience. The other is a better deal because it's full strength, so you get more."

That makes sense, I think, because a bottle of any full-strength concentrate is always going to equal more than the same size bottle of a diluted one, but I'm still confused about the whole diluting it thing. My husband took care of our vehicles. For thirty years, I never had to concern myself with automotive responsibilities. I saw him pour antifreeze directly into the radiator and just assumed that's what you did. I pick up the undiluted bottle to read the back, searching for instructions.

The clerk watches me from the end of the aisle. She says, "The undiluted stuff, that's just for older ladies who've lost their husband and don't know what to do."

I stand there, holding the container of antifreeze, staring at her, motion-less as a deer on a dark country road, blinded by headlights. Stunned. The instinct to flee from danger is frozen. I do not speak. My heart, which sits stationary in my chest, begins to race. I feel hot beneath my wool coat and begin to sweat. The woman can't hear the words that travel from my brain to my lips because they get lodged in my throat. *My husband died nine months ago today.* The awkwardness of my silent stare ushers a gust of rambling from her mouth that sounds like static. Then my capacity for flight returns. I place the undiluted antifreeze in the cart and head to checkout.

I can't get out of the store quick enough. With effort, I hold back my tears. I want to flee like a deer once released from the glare of high beams and bound into the shelter of tall grass on the side of the road and the trees be-yond. The line creeps.

Once I've paid, I sit in my car in the darkness of the winter evening. The sky is obscured by clouds. Undiluted grief lets loose as rain begins. Those words, "that's just for older ladies who've lost their husband and don't know what to do," knock hard against my skull. I don't know if I've bought the right kind of antifreeze. *Maybe I bought the wrong kind, maybe I should have gotten the diluted kind?* But that's not for middle-aged widows. I'm the wrong fucking demographic.

Antifreeze is essential for a vehicle to run properly. It lowers the freezing point of the liquid circulating the engine and prevents it from freezing in cold temperatures. It allows for flow, movement. In deep grief, time moves differently; it both halts and progresses simultaneously. Sometimes you feel stuck, like a fish caught still in ice, concentrated, and you think life will always be this way; you will never know another ounce of happiness again. Other times, tears flow undiluted, emotion rolls in waves, and even though you feel suspended on a floating grief cloud, it is moving through the sky, sifting past other clouds and mountain tops, over forests and meadows, drifting over neighborhoods and railroads and playgrounds.

I eat dinner at my favorite Japanese restaurant and have the first solid meal I've had in weeks: salad and rice and grilled mahi mahi. Nourishment helps ground me from the shock of the salesclerk's ill-fitting words. Afterward, as I drive the half-hour home to my little cabin in the woods, the rain falls steadily making visibility more difficult.

The rural roads of my small town are unlit, so it's necessary to use high beams at night. There is a car ahead, so I turn to the low beams. About four miles away from home, I approach a big curve, one that in winter exists in shadow and often is covered in ice that rarely thaws. But this night, it's raining, so there is no ice. I drive slowly around the curve. It is the curve that many years ago, as my husband and I were driving home late from a party, a gorgeous long-haired white cat streaked in front of our truck with no time to even hit the brakes before the horrific thud under the tires. Every time I drive this curve, I think about that cat.

The radio is playing something soulful and melancholy, like Van Morrison, which reinforces the tenderness from the earlier affront. The rain is sheeting, and I'm now on the straightaway. The car in front has sped ahead, but I keep my low beams on. I'm picking up speed after the curve, driving not fast, not slow, but steady at around forty miles per hour. In the narrowed light cast by the low beams, on the passenger side, a large brown dog with floppy ears, hound-like, bolts from the shadows, running at break-neck speed, ears flapping up and down so that I can see the pale underside in flickers. It is so close, two or three feet from the car. I slam on the brakes—BAM—the dog and the car collide with a walloping force. The car skids to a halt.

I pull over to the side of the road, turn off the car, but leave the headlights on. I fumble for my headlamp on the passenger seat, whimpering in a high-pitch cry, "no, no, no." I walk back toward the site of impact, searching the road in the dark in the rain, all the while crying that high-pitch cry. It is a moan really, like a wailing wind. The dog is nowhere to be seen. It has probably flown into the ditch or beyond, but I am so distraught I cannot think clearly to realize this.

A man comes out of the house across the street from where I've parked. He heads straight to my car, so I walk back toward it. In an accusatory and aggravated voice, he yells, "Did you hit something?"

I call out, "yes," but don't recognize my voice. It dips and rises, a high-pitched keening carried on the wind back to the car, to this unfamiliar man.

"What did you hit? What did you hit?" the man yells. He is an imposing shadow moving toward me in the dark in the rain on this sleepy rural road.

"A dog," I whimper in that same high-pitch tone. I'm bewildered and shaking—from the salesclerk's unforgettable words, from the sound of impact—BAM—hitting the dog, from being accosted by this man.

"That's my friend's dog!" the man yells. "It just got out! Where is it? Where is it?" He's practically in my face. There is something unhinged about this man. My amygdala is triggered. *Fight, flight, or freeze, fight, flight, or freeze.*

I point back down the road, still whimpering. He erupts in a profanity-laced tirade at the top of his lungs and heads in that direction.

I have a choice, much like the choice between diluted and undiluted antifreeze. I can remain frozen to the spot like a deer in headlights, the way I did in the aisle of Bi-Mart as I stared in disbelief at the salesclerk, or I can antifreeze—run like the dog with the wind nipping at its heels, sure and straight, with utter abandon, out of the darkness, toward a future however finite.

Without hesitation, I get in my car and drive.

Mail-Order Salve

Brenda Yates

Familiar markings—dark hair, wide
mouth, angular face, long-fingered

hands—now propelled by strangely-
moving limbs. As though a new

inhabitant with alien eyes had taken
up residence, the way a hermit crab

dons another creature's shell. Despite
swelling: complete physical recovery.

But cerebral hemorrhage squeezed out
time. And when you woke, childhood

had a face more familiar than your
wife's. Moving back to the comfort

of hometown sights and smells, you
send letters: page after page of memories

vivid as today. I'd almost forgotten
our summers spent roaming the woods

behind your house, how we captured
flying squirrels with fur softer than air

and all those days we spent swimming
the wide bay in front, in the water that

time and again revealed its blue magic
until our reddened eyes blurred.

humanitarian pause for humanitarian purposes

$$f(\textit{The Dow Jones gains 400 points})$$

$$= \frac{\textit{calling for a four} - \textit{day halt in fighting}}{\textit{Orthodox Christians' Holy Week} \times i} \pm$$

$$\frac{f(\textit{Noting that Orthodox Easter is coming})}{\textit{S\&P 500 now!} - \textit{is all the more urgent}}\,dx +$$

$$\sqrt{\textit{owing to the fact that}}$$

$$=$$

$$Z(\textit{Russian offensive}) = \frac{U.\,N.\,chief}{\sqrt{said\ldots}} \int_{-\infty}^{\infty} \frac{and^{-t^2}\,\textit{Macron, Biden,}\ldots}{t - said\ldots}$$

$$= i \int_{0}^{\infty} e^{-shi - t^2/4}\,dt$$

$$+$$

$$\sum a\ \textit{drops of ink}$$

pause

Radoslav Rochallyi

In the Name of the Name

Sunyoung Kay

Every winter, geese, instinct-driven,
　　　　rise up from waters. In spring they
　　　　　　　return, siren-called, to the pond in the same town
　　　　　　　　　　　they were born
　　　　　　　　　　　　　and their parents,
　　　　　　　　　　　and grandparents,
　　　　　　　　　to feather-lined nests –
　　My dad once played king in a palace of
marble and chandelier refractions,
　　　homeward night drives for a place to rest the
　　　　　　　　　　briefcase, and nap. I cried when this
　　　　　　　　　　　　stranger/father
　　　　　　held me. My mother painted the red brick
　　　fireplace white in the living room.
Only those who lived there noticed.
　　　　　　　　I flew on horses, coats like morning sun-stream waters.
　　　　Love written across the smile-crinkled dollar bill
of immigrant parents' American Dream.
　　　Good Asian men wear careers like laurels –
　　　　　　In the name of the name of the family name
　　　　　　　　defer life never lived before blaring blue and red
　　　　　　　　　sirens charioted away his crippling heart.
　　　　　　This year, geese return,
　　　pond, parking lot swallowed.
Flat feet slapping the blacktop,
　　　black eyes blinking
　　　　at pedestrians from drainage ditches.
　　　　　　"They'll move on," the nurse in blue scrubs says, *"to a new pond*
　　　　　　　　to something better."

Today, I march
to this building
that rises like a castle of mirror-gleam windows
where my dad once stayed
stomach stilled, putrid, black gunk
being drawn from a tube down his nose,
to witness the next thousand little drownings.

A History in Houses

Mary Liza Hartong

I've lived in nineteen houses, some beauties, some dumps. For example, when I was twenty-three, I paid three hundred dollars a month to live in a closet with a slanted ceiling. My roommate's cat would yowl through the hallways at night, especially on the nights she had a lover. I hung art. I made my bed. But the house had a shower that never seemed to drain, and after three months of going ankle deep in someone else's murky water and plugging my ears over the sound of the cat, I moved out.

On the other hand, when I was twenty-four, I lived in a house where I had a great big bedroom. I saw the seasons perform their tricks on the tree outside my window. Green to gold to white and then back to that meek kind of green that one day, out of nowhere, bursts with birds and life. In the mornings I would drink coffee with my roommate. Silly little pajamas, messy hair. We painted mugs at a pottery studio a few towns over, where you could get a plate of fries while you worked. Our mugs were flecked with salt. We were endlessly proud of them.

At twenty-five I lived in Ireland. It didn't rain as much as you would think. At twenty-six I lived in a shotgun house where there were always cockroaches in the kitchen. I would take long borrowed bike rides through the neighborhood, cruising for unwanted furniture. Coffee tables, saucepans. I furnished my apartment directly from the curb. Even the red patio chairs, which I propped up on the front porch beside the plants that wouldn't grow in the Louisiana heat, came from someone else's garbage. What I liked most about that house was my upstairs neighbor, who read palms and lent me her bike. She eventually left the neighborhood to have a baby, taking the charm with her, but not the bike.

The phases of my life ebbed and flowed from these nineteen houses. Each move meant the end of something—a bad roommate, a good view—but also the beginning. Isn't it comforting to know that for every slanted ceiling there is a room with a big window? That no matter how bad things get, you may still emerge, boxes piled high in the trunk of your car, from one life into the next? I recently saw a picture of the coffee house. The new tenants were smiling from the big, white couch where we used to talk in our pajamas. They looked so young. I wanted to warn them against apartments with cockroaches and sidewalks with cracks. But if I'm an expert in anything, it's that the lease will end. You will be both the taker of the red patio chairs and the one who leaves them behind. You will make it to house number nineteen and, because the tree outside your window has only just turned green, you will stay awhile.

Urban Scar

Patrick Horner

The building has a scar up its side. One day someone cut the building from top to bottom and the building's guts spilled onto the street and blood soaked the bricks, spattering and diffusing with the pouring rain. Hoards of bicycles passed trailing blood throughout the city. One night the residents stitched the building back up again and now it has a scar.

Urban Scar
oil on canvas
75 cm by 150 cm

Family Portrait
Ojo Taiye

My father is the man who will fall in the fall in the fallow field. Calling the past a small menace doesn't stop the hemorrhage. To read a poem is to follow a procession of soft, bright bursts. To write it is to be tired of women doing dishes. Today, every memory glistens with the dew of hunger. I have an aunt who won't get married. Trauma is to witness her body invaded by the thrust of men. Trauma is to know sex as the hands used to muffle her screams. The word strip is better as a noun than as a verb. I wish the night had not. I claim her my kin but her mouth still bleeds. To the river, every woman's cry is a plea for freedom. Most nights I calm myself by assigning her a hotline. The rain is just rain & a hurricane like a flashover grieves the center of her body. What if I can't stop licking her furs? It's possible that neither supplication nor streptomycin would save her. More than once, I kiss the fire at the end of the switch—the doctor asks if I know anything of clinical depression. I think of my sister, eleven & wed.

Outer Space Pioneer

Penny Page

The sun was setting, dragging long fingers of shadow down the folded rocky faces of the Santa Rosa Mountains on the northern side of the valley. Robby threw his sleeping bag, the one with the plaid flannel lining he'd had since high school, an unopened family-size bag of Doritos, and a one-gallon, rinsed-out milk container filled with water onto the passenger seat of his 1999 Toyota RAV-4. The righthand pocket of his cargo shorts sagged slightly with the weight of his lighter and loaded pot pipe, but he still placed his hand lightly against the lump to reassure himself he hadn't forgotten them.

The ignition of the RAV caught with a grind. Whatever that noise was, it would need repair at some point. More money he didn't have. He pulled away from his mother's three-bedroom rambler and sped down Frying Pan Road and past Flat Cat Canyon, his tires humming over the thin, splitting asphalt. Three minutes later, he reached the small town of Borrego Springs. As he passed his old high school, he stomped the gas to burn rubber, leaving exhaust fumes and black tire streaks in his wake.

Ninety-five percent of his classmates had gone west or east for better prospects after graduation. Only those who joined their family's local business, or dared to start their own enterprise, had stayed. Except for Robby. At twenty-eight, he still lived in the smallest of his mother's three bedrooms, the one at the end of the hall with a single, dirt-specked window smothered on the outside by overgrown oleanders that reached the roof. The tough, dense wall of vegetation blocked out the light, even at midday, and he liked it that way. The dimness allowed his eyes to gloss over the mattress on the floor, his scratched and nicked childhood dresser, and the second-hand desk with a broken drawer where he spent hours alone, hunched over his laptop surfing the net.

He zipped down Palm Canyon Drive and then took a sharp left onto Peg Leg Road, passing the perennial smattering of RVs boondocking on the flat, easily accessible desert terrain. He drove mindlessly, letting the warm desert air blow past his face through the open window, flying over a dip in the road so that his stomach rose and fell as the RAV caught air. When he reached Erosion Road and the Borrego Badlands, where narrow canyon-like gorges exposed the earth's history in colored layers of sediment and signs of civilization faded to nothing amid the ancient rock-strewn geography of the desert, he finally felt like he could breathe.

His mother's house had grown more stifling after Lloyd, his mom's boy-friend, had moved in nine months ago. Robby didn't dislike Lloyd, but he didn't like him either.

Lloyd managed a run-down RV park that kept him busy during the day, but he was at the house every evening and most weekends. When Robby complained that Lloyd had been scarfing up all the Doritos, cookies, and ice cream, his mother had retorted, "At least Lloyd pays rent and pitches in for food."

Robby, who could barely afford to put gas in his car, could think of no argument in response. He had no real job, unless you called occasionally working at Calico's sandwich shop a job. Last year he'd been fired for showing up, more than once, smelly and stoned, but the owners had been forced to hire him back to meet demand during the winter-spring tourist season when the hordes flocked over from San Diego to overrun the town and trample the desert blooms. Now that the suffocating heat of summer had arrived, his work had dried up, and with it, his funds. He was broke.

He sighed and pressed on past Coachwhip Canyon and the Calcite mine, either of which would be fine places to spend the night. Both were well-known, and even though he was currently the only car on the lonely road, chances were high that he'd meet other campers in those areas, and he wanted to avoid that. Tonight, like a cement block sinking to the bottom of the ocean, he wanted to drown himself in desert solitude, let it engulf him, take him away from his mother, away from Lloyd, and away from the landfill that was his life.

The Palo Verde Wash lay a few hundred yards ahead.

Reestablished yearly by seasonal flash flooding, the floor of the stony, sandy wash provided a drivable trail more than wide enough to accommodate Robby's RAV. At the turnoff, he slowed and drove off the asphalt and onto the wash, his tires swishing through the sand.

The RAV bumped and rocked from side to side as it rolled over basket-ball-sized boulders and sank into sandy depressions. A few dozen Palo Verde trees thrived along the wash border, beneficiaries of the intermittent rushing water, their hairy barbed needles glowing pea green in the beam of his headlights. The terrain was rough going for the RAV, but he drove on to where the wash cut between two low mud hills. Here, he parked and gathered his sleeping bag, water, and Doritos from the passenger seat, congratulating himself on remembering to grab the mini-mag flashlight from his glove box. He walked down the wash away from his car until he found a trail leading south.

The hiking trail ran diagonally up the side of a rounded hill. Despite the angle, the trail was steep. Climbing it was a struggle, and when he reached the top, he was winded and nearly crawling on all fours. He cursed his flabby gut and his fleshy out-of-shape legs.

He trekked another few hundred yards, pushing across the sand and stumbling over unseen rocks and stiff mounds of brittlebush.

Even with the mini flashlight, it was getting too dark for such arduous walking. He found a protected spot next to a waist-high boulder between two low rises and spread his sleeping bag on the sand. He tossed the bag of Doritos onto one side and placed the gallon of water on the other. He settled onto the flannel, leaning his back against the boulder that rushing water had deposited there eons ago, and fished the pot pipe and lighter out of his pocket. The burning grass glowed orange in the pipe's bowl as he lit up and took a big toke. He exhaled slowly, the odoriferous smoke snaking lazily into the warm air.

He wished he had his phone. The first two times he had dropped it, it had survived the impact, but the third time it hit the concrete with an ominous crack and went totally dead. He was unable to coax even a spark of life from behind the fractured screen, no matter how much he cursed and cajoled. He doubted the aging phone could be repaired. He'd be forced to buy a new one if he could save up the money, which might be never.

If he sold the RAV, he could buy a phone, but then he'd have no way to escape his mother's house, even temporarily. A better idea might be to buy a vehicle he could live in, like a van, a cool black one with teardrop windows and a plug-in cooler for pop and beer. He'd name his van Vanessa (ha) and live on the open road, surviving on fast food and short-term work. He'd meet other travelers, outsiders like him, with stories to share. He'd let them hitch a ride in Vanessa for a stretch and they'd be beholden to him for the transportation. They'd admire him for his nomadic ways, for his willingness to throw off the confines of a house, a job, a girlfriend; all the things that others seemed to step into so easily, all the things he was coming to understand he would never attain.

In his heart, he knew the dream of Vanessa would always remain unfulfilled. He'd never gather the ambition to strike out on his own. The rut he lived in was too deep and soft to crawl out of. So, if not Vanessa, then what? Was it too late to make a change? Had life passed him by?

He stretched out on the bag, took another toke, and gazed up at the stars. How he loved the night sky, the vast blackness of its depth, the final frontier, as James T. Kirk, Captain of the Starship Enterprise, had so aptly labeled it. The idea of flying through infinite space with stars flashing past, going to places no earthling had ever been, stirred within him a thrilling excitement he rarely felt.

An article in the most recent edition of the weekly Borrego Sun had caught his attention and his imagination. He'd read the short article so many times, he had it memorized.

"UFO Sighting—On June 14, around 9:15 p.m., an object was seen careening across the Borregan sky. Half the town must have seen it, as the sheriff's office was invaded by calls, and social media was alight. There have been a number of sightings recently, and one similar to this, thirteen miles south in Ranchita, about a month ago, but not as visual as this one."

That was part of why he was out here. Truthfully, he didn't expect to see anything more than stars, but he held a sliver of hope that he might catch a glimpse of whatever people had seen in the night sky. Sighting a UFO. How cool would that be? If he saw one, he'd run after it, try to flag it down, see if he could catch a ride.

He despised those rich assholes with their penis-shaped carnival-ride rockets, taking other rich assholes to the edge of Earth's atmosphere. Nothing more than buses on a circular route. And stuck on Mars with the Trumps and Musks and Bezoses of the world? No. Thank. You. He'd take his chances with the aliens. Although, it would be awesome to own a penis-shaped rocket.

He'd read that there were billions of planets.

Life was out there; he was sure of it. The desert was much like what a person might find on other planets, he imagined. Flat land, rocky hills dotted with scrub, and miles and miles of sand.

If he did make it into space, exploring other planets would not be his priority. Rather, he saw himself flying solo through the dark, airless vacuum, unencumbered by lack of light or atmosphere, mapping galaxies like an outer space pioneer. His body would need to be adapted, of course, upgraded into a vessel that could withstand such travel conditions. He wasn't afraid of that. Giving up his current physique would be a plus.

He'd already traveled through outer space many times in his mind. Space was never-ending and ever-expanding. This was hard to comprehend, but this is what would enable his important pioneering work to go on forever. It would be dark out there, but he was accustomed to the dark. He lived in a room with a window that light could not penetrate, a four-walled cave into which he retreated daily to escape his mother, a place where he could get stoned, lie on his mattress with the lights off, and let his mind float.

Over the nearest ridge, out of sight but not by far, a coyote's piercing howl split the night. Startled, Robby jerked and sat forward, his blood pumping. He wasn't afraid of coyotes. He could scare them off if he had to. They weren't fearless enough to mess with something as big as him when the desert was filled with jackrabbits, but that shriek had given him a good jolt. The volume still echoed in his ears. Those suckers were loud up close. He chuckled and relaxed back against the boulder.

An Elf Owl softly whoo-hooed from a Palo Verde tree in the wash behind him. He sat up again, suddenly energized. "Come and get me!" he shouted. He threw his head back and challenged the stars, "Here I am. Come and get me!"

Silence responded. He slumped back against the rock, crunched through half the bag of Doritos, then slugged a mouthful of water to wash it down. His eyes grew heavy. He gently cradled his pot pipe in his hand, its smooth glass and familiar shape as comforting as a childhood teddy bear. He stretched out on his sleeping bag and dozed until sometime later when a whirring hum woke him. More vibration than sound, it was soft yet loud, unrelenting yet soothing, a purr unnatural to the desert. He unstuck his dry tongue, still coated in orange Dorito powder, from the roof of his mouth and blinked to clear his vision.

A blue, dome-shaped glow shone above the nearest ridge.

He roused himself, rolled to his knees, and stood, light-headed for a moment. The whirring continued and the light remained, a steady shimmer of neon sapphire beneath the stars. He wasn't dreaming.

He wobbled away from his sleeping bag and toward the radiance as if called. Panting, he topped the crown of the ridge and saw it—a ship—round, and as big as his high school gymnasium. It hovered over the desert rocks. Blue fluorescent lights ringed its perimeter and highlighted the topography below like a theater stage. He tramped toward it hypnotized. This was it. They had heard him. They had come for him.

He stood beneath the ring of light and let the pot pipe slip from his fingers, marking his last stand on Earth. The illumination bathed his face as he gazed up at the ship's underbelly. A black circle the size of a manhole opened above him. A warm yellow beam surrounded him like a spotlight. His dusty sandalled feet lifted off the desert floor, and Robby was gone.

***

At ten the next morning, Robby's mom, without knocking, opened the door to his room to rouse him for breakfast. He would sleep all day if she let him. She saw his bed, a tangled mess as usual, but this morning he was not part of the tangle, which was unusual. She wandered back to the living room and separated the sheer curtains, stirring up drifting dust particles. She squinted out at the cement driveway where the temperature had already risen to over eighty degrees under the uncompromising sun. Robby's RAV wasn't there.

She yelled over her shoulder to Lloyd, who was in the bathroom finishing his morning ablutions, the door half-closed. "Where did Robby say he was going?"

Lloyd grunted and then yelled back, "Heck if I know." The toilet flushed, and Lloyd joined her at the window. "Don't worry. He's a big boy. He'll find his way."

A tale of two sneakers

Jasmine Harrell

A pair of weather-beaten shoes dangling over a powerline
Tells the quiet story of their slow demise:
"Our owner got cornered by a gang of bullies.
They beat his stomach blue and his face raw.
Lumps rose like mountains after violent quakes.
They took from him the grace of staggering home,
In snatching us from his feet.
They bound us by string in a tight knot
And threw us upward.
We gagged upon our sharp descent on
The wire. Our bodies slammed against each
Other and then we just swayed.
Nauseous, dizzy, frightened.
If we had necks they would have snapped on impact.
And all we could do was watch our owner limp home,
His poor feet twitching in pain as glass and stone
Scattered across the ground
Sunk into his soles,
Adding low blows he could barely avoid
In that bubble of shame."

How Busy I Was

Marjorie Drake

Crazy busy

There's not enough time in the day.

I never *stop*—I have *so* much to do every day, and there's always more that needs to be done the next day and the day after that.

But I'm the early bird and I have a substantial clew of worms, wriggling in a magnificent fat ball, demonstrating my dominance in the lawyering business.

Crazy *busy*

There are two kinds of people: Those who, on snowy mornings, roll over in bed, pleased to have an excuse to be tardy. And those of us who make sure the night before that the snowblower's working and gassed up, and set the alarm an hour early so no time is wasted.

The somnolent slackers become the prey of the African wild dogs—the butchers. They rid the community of the weak.

And thereby improve the species.

Crazy busy

Who needs sleep, amiright? I've trained myself to sleep only six hours and hope to reduce that number. Multi-tasking is my superpower— I'm raising it to an art form. Which is a damn good thing because there are clients to call, files to open, meetings to attend, emails to answer, motions to file, trials to prepare for, letters to write, and, most importantly, checks to collect. And in *our* business, we eat what we kill, including—like cannibal creatures such as sharks, pigs, earwigs and snakes—our own.

Crazy Busy!

Adrenaline is a drug, the hustle a pleasure, being quick on your feet a necessity—I like to fuck 'em on the stand and watch the color bleed from the face into the neck when realizing their lies have been exposed.

Some find meerkats cuddly and lovable. Their timidity disgusts me.

CRAZY BUSY!

Adrenaline is a drug, the best—but sometimes the adrenal glands don't produce enough to meet the needs of the day. That's why Adderall was invented—to help me manage the demands of my life. Unlike its illegal cousin, methamphetamine, Adderall is a safe form of additional energy and focus, and it's legal—well, we got it legally for our son and he won't take it, and I won't tolerate waste. Naturally, an antidote is necessary when dosages are misjudged or the effects overstay their welcome. Weed is an unacceptable option—I am an officer of the court, after all. In addition, it induces apathy and sloth. Bourbon, on the other hand, is the perfect solution, a legal and effective anesthetic rapidly producing adequate tension relief to permit the required hours of sleep (now down to five!) before rejoining the race in the morning. No hibernation, no gorging, no long months of torpor like the hedgehogs and the bears; nor the lethargic stages of snake brumation. Just cat naps, a quick rest before returning to the battle.

CRAZY BUSY!!

I've taken one vacation in five years, and spent a lot of time answering emails on the beach. It's hard to do in the sun; you'd think Apple would create a better screen for using the i-phone in sunlight. But there'll be plenty of time for vacations later—and the means to go to more exotic places—where we'll dive into azure waters to spear lionfish in Belize, shoot leopards and elephants on an African safari, and dine in France on the savory ortolan bunting, crunching their fragile skeletons against the roofs of our mouths.

Still Very Busy

Which is good, of course. But the years do take a toll. I'm a very senior partner now, with a great deal of power and influence. Trials aren't the best use of my time at this point, however. I throw myself with equal vigor into the necessary functions of mentoring the associates and maintaining relationships with our important clients.

I'm the top rainmaker in the firm. And I train the up-and-comers, the young red-hots panting to do some "fuckin' 'em on the stand" of their own. They never tire of my instructive stories—how to snatch victory from your opponent by a well-timed procedural maneuver; how to build your billables with ten-hour depositions and meaningless motions; how to make litigation so expensive that your opponent withdraws the case in exchange for you agreeing not to sue them for filing such an audacious lawsuit.

I'm still a lion of the bar—the king of the jungle, my strengths now put to a different, and equally important use.

Kinda Busy

Sometimes there *are* moments of fatigue—not unexpected for a man about to begin his eighth decade. I'm drowsy at the moment in fact, though I've barely taken a sip of this bottled-in-bond bourbon I save for a convivial Friday afternoon libation with partners, or a reward for an especially precocious associate.

My girl, typing quietly in the hall outside my office, looks up at me. I remove my feet from the desktop and straighten my shoulders.

I *will* rest my head on my desk—for just a second. I'm a little dizzy, and that gnawing pain in my shoulder is worsening, spreading into my chest. I sit up, try to catch my breath. *Damn.*

There's Philip, a year younger than me and not nearly as productive, peering in. Hairless, with that beak under beady eyes—trained on me like a vulture. He's always wanted this twenty-fifth floor corner office. I want to make a joke—"I'm not dead yet, Philip!" I open my mouth, but no sound is emitted. More people now crowd around my door, and into my office. There's a high buzz of sound, but I can't understand anything.

Not so busy

And then, they're lifting me onto the stretcher, and I see the view through the window behind my desk—the silver and gold of the shiny highrises glinting in the setting sun, the red and purples just beginning to fade into pink and lilac.

And Philip sitting in my chair! He pours bourbon into my glass, raises the glass, and our eyes meet fleetingly just before darkness descends.

Deity

Mitchell Untch

"Every one of the angels is terrifying."
                    Rilke

I asked my angel   Father
creator
forge me an unending river
a body flying through rivers
the way light glides through rivers
river-wind breaking ice
arms outstretched let go
shuddering clouds
wings shredded
illuminating sky

unearthing tributes to   Father
mother
sunlight breaking branches
leaves fastened to
Golden Rain, Silk Cotton
harboring light
fastened to earth
I asked him
angel

                                                                        Father

creator
make me the river
rain-played over and over and over
not knowing how my head of blond hair
would surface depthless
my face an unmasked stream
a body rifling
what sky loves

already flown darkening
becoming my   Father
giving birth to nothing
and everything
inside him
adrift
hammering
hands blackening my face
nights leaving my body
a field of mauled iris
upturned stones eyes widening
as I dream of how *he* once might have dreamed of flying
wind spread over his arms
angel   Father
creator
how he had molded his body into mine
a face, blank
staring back at me crying out
lucent as starlings
too late too late too late too late
his voice emptied inside me
a bell a wrung fist
mirror in the Garden angel   Father
creator

without mercy.

Errata for My Unfinished Biography

Adrian S. Potter

p. 6, in the fourth sentence, before the word *childhood*, replace the word *quiet* with *awkward* or *disarranged*.

p. 36 and **p. 73**, in the paragraphs bookending the adolescent years, replace all subjunctive verbs with words that reflect remorse for what I should have tried, or better, embarrassment for not trying at all.

p. 107, After my father passed, the smirking professor's remark that I *made up his death to weasel out of finals* was unfounded, and thus the second paragraph should read:

> *After the test, the tequila and whiskey, their sting and sour, poured smooth and somewhat pleasurably into my mouth. A grieving mind embraces vices while searching for relief, ready to plunge into error, to prevent getting pulled apart like a wishbone. Knuckles pop to the pressure of post-exam jitters as a paternal ghost haunts the corners of a barroom.*

p. 125, third paragraph, sixth line, *tend to see the good in people* should read *am prone to loving trainwrecks, or becoming one myself.*

> [This erratum more accurately reflects a debt to the co-authors of *My Divorce* and *Toxic Relationship #8* than to the books currently cited in Appendix C (missing).]

p. 166, first paragraph, second line, after the semi-colon, replace the phrase *in the morning* with *after four hours of threadbare sleep.*

p. 204, left column, replace all bulleted items with an inventory of moments when I observed or experienced discrimination yet stayed situationally silent, or a catalog of times when dangerous things accidentally got paired together, such as dulled hopes with sharp objects.

p. 268, after the fifth sentence, add the following statement:

The stranger with whom I'm workshopping poems says I'd be capable of great things if only I didn't hold back.

Appendix E, at the end of the section entitled *Repeated Mistakes*, replace *half-hearted apologies* with *sincere regrets*. Wherever logical, add the prefix un- to each adjective or verb listed.

Bacopa Poets & Writers

2022

Alphabetical List of 2022 Contributors, *Bacopa Literary Review*

Dror Abend-David is worth three and a half books and some of articles, and can be exchanged for two camels and a goat. He has a thick skin, a big head, and a chip on his shoulder. He is over qualified, overreaching, over selling, overzealous, overworked, over acting, over the hill, and overdoing it.

John Agbaeze is an Igbo writer and a Geography graduate at The University of Nigeria, Nsukka. He has only a handful of unpublished pieces and lives in the city of Aba in an apartment he shares with a sister and another family. He is on Instagram @westkal.

David M. Alper's forthcoming poetry collection is *Hush*. His work appears in *Invisible City*, *Unbound Brooklyn*, *Mortal Mag*, and elsewhere. He teaches in New York City.

Lilia Snowfield Anderson was named after a great-great-uncle she never met. Bartending shifts consume her nights and her debut novel draft consumes her days. She lives in a small, Minnesota lake town. Her fiction can be found in *The Marrs Field Journal*, *The Agapanthus Collective*, *Blood & Bourbon*, and more.

Sarpong Osei Asamoah is a Ghanaian writer. He writes in Twi and English. He is featured in *Agbowo Magazine*, *Olongo Africa Magazine*, *Lolwe Magazine*, at WriteGhana.com, & more

Roxanne Barbour started writing after she took early retirement in 2010. Roxanne has published numerous novels: *An Alien Collective*, *Revolutions*, *Sacred Trust*, *Kaiku*, *Alien Innkeeper*, *An Alien Confluence*, and *Alien Innkeeper on Particle*. She also writes speculative poetry and has poems published in *Scifaikuest*, *Star*Line*, *Polar Borealis*, *Polar Starlight*, and other magazines.

Deviant Bates is a Texan-Taiwanese writer and poet. Their work reflects upon their experiences regarding madness, grief, and faith. Their work has found homes with *Delicate Friends*, *Poetry Online*, and others. They can be found on Twitter @darlingknife.

Greg Bell has written all his life as a necessity. His recent awakening to publishing found homes for some of his work in literary journals and anthologies,. He is a recipient of the 2019 Kowit Poetry Prize. He has author of the hybrid poetry collection *Looking for Will: My Bardic Quest with Shakespeare*.

Taras Bereza has worked as a freelance contributing writer since 2006. He is working as a lexicographer at Apriori Publishers, with 10 published dictionaries.

Maroula Blades is an Afro-British writer/artist living in Berlin. She was selected for the INITIAL Special Grant from the Academy of Arts in Berlin. In 2020, Chapeltown Books published her story collection, "The World in an Eye." Her works are published in numerous magazines and anthologies at home and abroad.

Abigail Boyer is currently a student at the University of Connecticut where she is currently majoring in English and American Studies. She hopes to eventually work in the journalism field to combine her love of writing with interest in politics.

Lawrence Bridges ' poetry has appeared in *The New Yorker, Poetry*, and *The Tampa Review*. He has published three volumes of poetry: *Horses on Drums* and *Flip Days* with Red Hen Press and *Brownwood* with Tupelo Press. You can find him on IG: @larrybridges

Trista Cornelius is a writer and artist in Portland, Oregon. Previously, as an English Instructor, Trista helped writers build confidence and find their voices, and she hopes her essays make people feel less alone, more connected, and less "freakish" as Phillip Lopate said of essay writing.

B. Elliot Crist was an English teacher in a former life, who started painting in 1976 and was first published in 1984. He was most recently witnessed as Emmitt Smith's dancing partner on Dancing with the Stars. His paintings and his poetry are of the Absurd Impressionist school.

Rivka Crowbourne is a Catholic poet and aspiring mother who wishes you infinitely well.

Arthur Crummer, musician, poet, and novelist, earned degrees in Engineering mathematics to support those habits. He wrote the novels *Wrestling God* and *Floating Island*, the poetry chapbook *Almost Everywhere Convergent*, original songs, instructional booklets on guitar and Dobro, and produced a couple of music CDs. Art was the second president of Writers Alliance of Gainesville.

Eric Diamond is a psychotherapist, men's work leader, guitarist, songwriter, and poet; (self)-published *Strange Frontier*, *Hold this Goblet*, and *Always Take Door Number Three*.

Jeffrey Dieter's work has appeared in *Allegheny Review*, *Barrier Island Review*, *Calliope*, *Grubb Street*, Harford Poetry and Literary Society, *The Hollins Critic*, *River Poets*, *Tributaries*, *Gertrude Press* and *Zillah*. He has also had the great fortune of winning 2nd place in the Bethesda Urban Literary Contest, judged by Stanley Plumly.

Marjorie Drake, after more than thirty years practicing law in Hartford, Connecticut, recently closed her practice to concentrate on her writing. Her work has appeared in *Parhelion Literary Magazine*, *Grey Sparrow Journal*, *Five on the Fifth*, and elsewhere.

Laurie Easter is the author of *All the Leavings* (Oregon State University Press). Her work has been anthologized and published widely, including in *Brevity*, *The Rumpus*, *Sweet Lit*, and *Hippocampus Magazine*, among others. She lives off the grid in Southern Oregon.

Tyler Fisher, of Ojibwe (Chippewa) heritage, is a professor of modern languages at the University of Central Florida, where he has the privilege of teaching interdisciplinary courses on Creativity and Narrative. His book-length translations of poetry include José Martí's *Ismaelillo* (Wings Press 2007) and Federico Garcia Lorca's *The Dialogue of Two Snails* (Penguin 2018).

Ashley Guadamuz is a recent graduate of Southern New Hampshire University who majored in Creative Writing. She completed her Master's Capstone focusing on cultural identity, and the poem "Feliz Cumpleaño" in this issue reflects her passion to discover herself within Latin America.

James Hancock is a writer/screenwriter of thriller, horror, fantasy, sci-fi, bizarre comedy and twisted fairy tales. A few of his short screenplays have been made into films, and he has been published in print magazines, online, and in anthology books. He lives in England, with his wife and two daughters.

Jasmine Harrell says writing is one of her passions. She graduated from Bowie State University with a degree in English and a concentration in Creative Writing. She then worked hard to become an Editor and used part of that income to fund her writing career.

Mary Liza Hartong lives and writes in her hometown of Nashville. Her work has appeared in *StyleBlueprint*, *Lascaux Review*, *Ember Chasm Review*, *Saturday Evening Post*, *FiveSouth*, and more. A proud aunt and enthusiastic Dartmouth grad, she spends her non-writing hours telling stories to her five adorable nieces.

Taiwo Hassan is a writer of Yorùbá descent, a poet and a vocalist. A Best of The Net Nominee, his poems have appeared in *trampset* and several other places. His first chapbook, *Birds Don't Fly for Pleasure* is forthcoming for publication by River Glass Books.

Karin Hedetniemi is a writer, poet, and street photographer from Vancouver Island, Canada. Her creative work is published in *Prairie Fire, Hinterland, MORIA*, and other literary journals. In 2020, Karin won the nonfiction prize from the Royal City Literary Arts Society. Find her at AGoldenHour.com or Twitter @karinhedet.

Silke Heiss is a South African writer who has published poems, short stories and a serialized verse novel in local literary journals and anthologies. She co-authored eight self-published books with her late husband, the poet Norman Morrissey, and has two solo poetry collections to her name. She is a member of the Ecca Poets and has collaborated on nine books with them to date.

Patrick Horner is a Canadian poet and engineer living in Copenhagen, Denmark, where he works to develop new water treatment technology. He co-wrote and co-produced Waste Dump, a serial radio play, and his poetry and fiction have been published in *Wax, Dandelion, Broken Pencil*, and more. His first book of poetry, *Refugia*, will be published by the University of Calgary Press in the fall of 2022.

HC Hsu 許翔程 is author of the short story collection *Love Is Sweeter* (Lethe) and essay collection *Middle of the Night* (Deerbrook). He has written for *Pif, Big Bridge, Iodine, nthposition, 100 Word Story, China Daily News, Epoch Times, Words Without Borders*, and many others. His translation of 2010 Nobel Peace Prize laureate Liu Xiaobo's biography, *Steel Gate to Freedom*, was published by Rowman & Littlefield in 2015.

Olaitan Humble is a writer and editor. He has been nominated for the Rhysling Award, Pushcart Prize and Best of the Net Award. His writing appears in *North Dakota Quarterly, FIYAH, HOBART, HOAX, Chiron Review, Superstition Review, Ethel Zine,* and *Luna Luna Magazine*, among others. Twitter: @olaitanhumble.

Sunyoung Kay is a poet located near St. Louis, Missouri who is just beginning the journey of revealing the stories held within.

Kateri Kosek's poetry and essays have appeared in *Orion, Creative Nonfiction, Briar Cliff Review, Terrain,* and other journals. She holds an MFA from Western Connecticut State University, teaches college English, and lives in western Massachusetts. She has been a resident at Kimmel Harding and the Tallgrass Artist Residency in Kansas.

Neethu Krishnan is a writer from Mumbai, India. She holds postgraduate degrees in English and Microbiology and writes between genres at the moment. Her work has appeared in *The Spectacle* and is forthcoming in *Seaside Gothic* and the anthology "*Dark Cheer: Cryptids Emerging*" (Volume Silver) from Improbable Press.

Peggy Landsman is the author of two poetry chapbooks, *Our Words, Our Worlds* (Kelsay Books, 2021) and *To-wit To-woo* (Foothills Publishing, 2008). Her work appears in many anthologies and journals. She lives in South Florida where she swims in the warm Atlantic Ocean every chance she gets. https://peggylandsman.wordpress.com

Diane LeBlanc is a writer, teacher, and book artist with roots in Vermont, Wyoming, and Minnesota. She is the author of *The Feast Delayed* (Terrapin Books, 2021) and four poetry chapbooks. Poems, essays, and reviews appear in numerous literary magazines. Diane is a holistic life coach with an emphasis in creative practice. She teaches at St. Olaf College in Northfield, Minnesota. Read more at www.dianeleblancwriter.com.

Miki Lentin completed an MA in Creative Writing at Birkbeck, was a finalist in the 2020 Irish Novel Fair for *Winter Sun*, placed highly in competitions including Fish Publishing and Leicester Writers, and published in *Litro*, *Storgy*, *Story Radio*, and *MIR*, among others. Miki volunteers with the refugee charity Breaking Barriers and with foodkind in Greece, and dreams of one day running a café again.

Jiewei Li 李劼韦 is a Chinese poet under lockdown in Shanghai that has a Creative Writing MA from Lancaster University and whose work has appeared in the online Art Journal, *The Scriblerus*.

Cassandra Lipp is co-producer of the Oddheader YouTube channel and former managing editor of *Writer's Digest*. Her work has been published in *Greener Pastures Magazine*, *Little Old Lady Comedy*, The *Belladonna*, *Points in Case*, and *Ohio's Best Emerging Poets*.

Olumide Manuel is a poet, environmentalist, and biology teacher. He takes inspiration from his immediate and personal realities and fantasies which include the magic forest house in his head.

Ted Marcelo, raised by proud Peruvians, writes from a first-generation American perspective. During the day, he works on instructional design for a sustainability nonprofit. In the late afternoon, he consumes media to the point of dissociation. At night, he dreams of rhyming to justify his English degree.

Hannah Marshall lives in Northeast Florida and spends her days fawning over her fruit trees so that they may someday grow into a food forest in which she can write poems and eat fresh citrus.

Julie McNeely-Kirwan's fiction and poetry have appeared in *Every Writer's Resource*, *Every Day Fiction*, *Overtime*, *Show Us Your Shorts*, *Prescription Playful*, and

They Call Us, among other sites/magazines. Currently, she lives in Arkansas with two elderly rescue dogs.

Karla Linn Merrifield has 15 books to her credit, including her new full-length poetry collection published in December 2021; it's titled *My Body the Guitar*, from Before Your Quiet Eyes Publications Holograph Series, which has been nominated for the 2022 National Book Awards. https://www.karlalinnmerrifield.org/

Jill Michelle teaches at Valencia College in Orlando, Florida. Her recent poems appear in *DMQ Review*, *Please See Me*, *untethered magazine*, *The Elevation Review*, *Bacopa Literary Review*, *Coffee People*, and elsewhere. Check out more of her work at byjillmichelle.com.

Cecil Morris retired after 37 years of teaching English, and now he tries writing himself what he spent so many years teaching others to understand and (maybe) enjoy. He has poems appearing in *Cobalt Review*, *Ekphrastic Review*, *Evening Street Review*, *Midwest Quarterly*, *Poem*, *Talking River Review*, and other literary magazines.

Michael Nethercott has authored two mysteries, *The Séance Society* and *The Haunting Ballad*, and a Western to be published next year. His stories have appeared in *Alfred Hitchcock Mystery Magazine*, *Magazine of Fantasy and Science Fiction*, and *Best Crime and Mystery Stories of the Year*.

J. Nishida is a Gainesville poet, writer, editor, tutor, sometimes teacher, and mom. She is one of the hosts of the Thursday Night Poetry Jam at the CMC. She enjoys travel and theatre; studying literature, linguistics, languages, mythology, and fairy tales; and annoying other poets with her experimental poetry.

Shauna Osborn is Executive Director of Puha Hubiya (an Indigenous arts non-profit). Their poetry collection *Arachnid Verve* was a finalist for an Oklahoma Book Award. Other honors include a New Poets of Native Nations Scholarship, a Crescendo Poetry Fellowship, and a National Poetry Award from the New York Public Library.

Jennifer Overturf's mother instilled in her a love of growing things that consumes her free time to this day.

Penny Page is a writer, a reader, a gardener, and a dog lover. She writes primarily paranormal and gritty off-beat stories. Her writing includes a self-published novella titled Not Haunted. She was a university administrator for twenty-five years and now happily writes full-time.

Roberta Pearla has a Masters in Education, Guidance and Counseling. She is also Certified in Language Arts and Gifted Education. She has been trained as a mentor and facilitator in Pongo Poetry, facilitating therapeutic writing through poetry. She has been awarded for her collage artwork, has had several poems published, and has created performances for poetry readings.

Marisca Pichette's work has appeared in *Strange Horizons*, *Fireside Magazine*, *Room Magazine*, *Ligeia Magazine*, *SNACK*, and *Plenitude Magazine*, among others. She lives in Western Massachusetts, collecting bones and listening to the trees.

Frederick Pollack is the author of two book-length narrative poems, THE ADVENTURE and HAPPINESS (Story Line Press; the former reissued 2022 by Red Hen Press), and two collections, A POVERTY OF WORDS (Prolific Press, 2015) and LANDSCAPE WITH MUTANT (Smokestack Books, UK, 2018). He has many other poems in print and online journals.

Adrian S. Potter is winner of the 2022 *Lumiere Review* Prose Contest and author of the poetry collection *Everything Wrong Feels Right* (Portage Press). Some past or forthcoming publication credits include *North American Review*, *Obsidian*, *Paper Dragon*, *The Comstock Review*, and *The Maine Review*. Visit him online at http://adrianspotter.com.

Kyle Potvin's debut full-length poetry collection is *Loosen* (Hobblebush Books, 2021). Her chapbook, *Sound Travels on Water*, won the Jean Pedrick Chapbook Award. She's a two-time finalist for the Howard Nemerov Sonnet Award. Poems have appeared in *Bellevue Literary Review, Tar River Poetry, Rattle, Ecotone*, and The New York Times.

Radoslav Rochallyi, PhD, is a Czech-based artist—philosopher, writer, painter, poet—a member of Mensa and of The Royal Society of Literature in the United Kingdom, and author of 14 books. He has presented visual work internationally, his math-visual works have been accepted in many institutions/galleries, and his visual poetic equations published in many journals at Stanford University, California State University, Dixie State University, Olivet College, and Las Positas College).

Paula M. Rodriguez is an educator in greater Los Angeles. She started her literary career in Spain, where she won a literary prize and published her work in academic journals. After migrating to the United States, she has focused on poetry and narrative.

J. Paul Ross is a graduate of Metropolitan State University of Denver. His fiction has appeared in numerous online and print journals.

Robert Sachs' fiction has appeared in *The Louisville Review*, *Chicago Quarterly Review*, *Free State Review*, *Great Ape Journal*, and *Delmarva Review*, among others. He holds an MFA in Creative Writing from Spalding University. His story "Vondelpark," was nominated for a Pushcart Prize in 2017; "Yo-Yo Man" was a Fiction Finalist in the 2019 Tiferet Writing Contest, and "Old Times" was Fiction Winner in the 2021 Tiferet Writing Contest. More at www.roberthsachs.com.

Piper Samuels is a young writer based in Los Angeles and Berkeley, CA. She attends UC Berkeley and is pursuing a Bachelor's degree in Media Studies with a minor in Creative Writing. Her experimental free verse poetry explores youth and age, focusing on the ways in which the childhood mind grows with time.

Angeline Schellenberg is the author of the Manitoba Book Award-winning *Tell Them It Was Mozart* (Brick Books, 2016) and the elegy collection *Fields of Light and Stone* (University of Alberta Press, 2020), finalist for the 2022 KOBZAR Book Award. Angeline hosts Speaking Crow, Winnipeg's longest-running poetry open mic.

Catherine Shields writes about parenting, disabilities, and self-discovery. In her debut memoir *The Shape of Normal* (Vine Leaves Press 2023), Catherine explores the truths and lies parents tell themselves. She resides in Miami, Florida with her husband who she's been married to forever. They enjoy taking long bike rides and kayaking in Biscayne Bay. Follow her on Instagram @cathyshieldswriter.

Murzban F. Shroff is a Mumbai-based writer. His fiction has appeared in 75 literary journals. He is the winner of the John Gilgun Fiction Award and has seven Pushcart Prize nominations. His short story collection, *Breathless in Bombay*, was shortlisted for the Commonwealth Writers' Prize and rated by the Guardian as among the ten best Mumbai books. His collection, *Third Eye Rising*, was featured on the *Esquire* list of Best Books of 2021. His novel, *Waiting for Jonathan Koshy*, was a finalist for the Horatio Nelson Fiction Prize and will be published in the U.S. in Fall 2022.

Sydney Sinks is a writer who likes coffee, cats, and cardigans. Her writing has also been featured in *The Decaturian, BURST Magazine, Gateway Journalism Review, Remington Review*, and *Decatur Magazine*. Follow her work on Twitter @SinksSydney.

Victoria Lynn Smith writes short stories, essays, and articles. She has been published on Brevity Blog, Wisconsin Public Radio, Moving Lives Minnesota, *Better Than Starbucks, 8142 Review, Red Cedar Review, Spring Thaw, Hive Literary Journal, Persimmon Tree, and Jenny*. Read more at writingnearthelake.org.

Kelley Swan's writing has appeared in literary journals such as *GUD Magazine, THEMA Literary Journal*, and *PiF Magazine*. After a quarter-century Gap Year, she's returned to college and is currently studying creative writing at the University of South Florida.

Ojo Taiye is an emerging artist and a dreamer. As someone who believes in the power of language, he is always investigating the imaginative potential of poetry to capture the minutiae of daily life and the natural world. Alongside working for a rural hospital, Taiye is a freelance writer for multiple magazines. and organizations. His poetry "muses on power struggles, race and culture, the damage of capitalism, and the tender fragility of hope."

Sylvia Anne Telfer is an international award-winning Scottish poet/short story writer frequently published in anthologies and magazines, a qualified English teacher, and one of her jobs was In-House Publications Manager at the University of Hong Kong. She is a campaigner to halt climate change, a feminist, and an equal rights activist.

R. Thursday (they/them) is a writer, historian, educator, and all-around nerd. When not subverting middle school social studies curriculum, they can be found reading, playing video games, or writing about space, vampires, comic books, queerness, and on good days, all of the above.

Mitchell Untch is an emerging writer. Publications include *Paris American*, *Moth*, *Fjords*, *Telluride Institute*, and *West Trade Review*, among others, as well as Telluride Institute Fischer Prize 2022 Finalist, *Crab Orchard Review* Book Contest 2017, The Journal: Wheeler Prize for Poetry 2018 Finalist, and two-time Pushcart Nominee.

Karla Van Vliet's newest books are *She Speaks in Tongues* (Anhinga Press), poems and asemic writings, and *Fluency: A Collection of Asemic Writings* (Shanti Arts.) She is a Forward Prize, three-time Pushcart Prize, and Best of the Net nominee. Van Vliet is a co-founder and editor of *deLuge Journal*.

Alla Vilnyanskaya was born in the Ukraine and raised in the U.S. She came to Philadelphia in 1989 with her parents. She holds an MA from Miami University and an MFA from Columbia University. Her work has been published in several online and print journals. She is currently working on her first full length book of poetry.

Ann Weil writes at the corner of Stratford and Avon in Ann Arbor, Michigan, and at Snipe's Point Sandbar off Key West, Florida. Her poems appear in *Crab Creek Review*, *Whale Road Review*, *Shooter Literary Magazine*, *Indianapolis Review*, and elsewhere. Visit her at www.annweilpoetry.com.

Robert Witmer has resided in Japan for more than 40 years. Now an emeritus professor, he has had the opportunity to teach courses in poetry, including haiku, not only at his home university in Tokyo but also in India. He has published a collection of haiku titled *Finding a Way*.

Brenda Yates is a Los Angeles resident and the prize-winning author of *Bodily Knowledge* (Tebot Bach) with poems, reviews, interviews and hybrids published in journals and anthologies based in Australia, Canada, China, England, India, Ireland, Israel, Japan, the Netherlands, and Portugal, as well as the United States

Bacopa Editors
2022

Editor in Chief J.N. Fishhawk is a poet and freelance writer. He is the author of two poetry chapbooks and *Postcards from the Darklands*, ekphrastic poems accompanying artwork by artist Jorge Ibanez. Fishhawk and illustrator Johnny Rocket Ibanez published their first-in-a-series children's book *Billy & Tugboat SallyForth* in 2020. Info at fishhawkandrocket.com.

Associate Editor Mary Bast's creative nonfiction, poetry, and flash memoir have appeared in a number of print and online journals, and she's author, co-author, or contributor to eight professional books from her career as a psychologist, leadership consultant, and Enneagram coach. Bast is also a visual artist.

Managing Editor Tessa Walters is a poet, writer, and songwriter living amongst the orange trees. They enjoy writing anything from poetry to fiction to plays. Whether they're recording original songs in the voice notes on their phone, hosting a Poetry Jam at the CMC, cuddling up with a library book, baking bread or pulling needle through thread, Tessa is presently enjoying life as a rebel without a clue.

Fiction Editor Alec Kissoondyal is a student at the University of Florida currently pursuing an undergraduate degree in English. He is also a writer for *Narrow Magazine* and an ambassador for the Florida Hemingway Society. His short story, 'Smudge', was published in the 2021 issue of *Bacopa Literary Review*. He has forthcoming publications to be released in *Drunk Monkeys Magazine*, *The Bookends Review*, and *The Underground*.

Creative Nonfiction and Humor Editor Stephanie Seguin studied English Literature and French at the University of Florida. She has published humor, short fiction, and personal memoir and spent over 15 years as a freelance editor and teacher of languages.

Poetry Co-Editor Oliver Keyhani is a visual and performance artist, poet and writer. He spends his time wondering about the spirits that put objects around us that cause us to stub our toes and funny bones, or those ghosts that pull out the chairs from under us just as we are about to sit. He can be found studying things and drinking hot chocolate.

Poetry Co-Editor Reinfred Dziedzorm Addo is a Ghanaian-American writer. He is the author of the poetry collections *Washed Over...Or, Things Dedicated* and *The Dedicadas: A Chapbook* (shortlisted for the GAW Literary Awards). In addition to winning awards such as the Nan Lacy Poetry Chapbook Contest, his work, including his health humanities creative writing, has been published in various publications and by various organizations such as *Tampered Press* and *Signs of Life: An Anthology*. Reinfred's favorite poetry communities in Gainesville are Thursday Night Poetry Jam (at the Civic Media Center), ART -SPEAKS, and Dopen Mic.

BACOPA *Literary Review* 2022

Designed by Richard Skinner
(delanoir2@gmail.com)

Fonts:

Calisto MT: an old-style serif typeface designed for the Monotype Corporation foundry in 1986 by Ron Carpenter, a British typographer, Calisto MT is intended to function as a typeface for both body text and display text.

Adobe Jensen Pro: an old-style serif typeface drawn for Adobe Systems by its chief type designer Robert Slimbach, Adobe Jensen Pro's Roman styles are based on a textface cut by Nicolas Jenson in Venice around 1470; its italics are based on those created by Ludovico Vicentino degli Arrighi fifty years later.